cold, thin air

A Collection of Disturbing Narratives and Twisted Tales

C.K. Walker

ISBN-13: 978-1502780126

ISBN-10: 1502780127

Table of Contents

BETSY THE DOLL

Like most people these days, I had a fucked up childhood. Who doesn't, right? My father took off before I was born and my mother was left to care for me on her own, a skill she was sorely lacking. My mother slipped right back into the drug-addled, party lifestyle she'd enjoyed before I was born and had soon turned our two-bedroom apartment into an opium den. For the first five years of my life, I walked around in a confused, terrifying mist. The smoky air would flood down the hallway from our living room and slip under my bedroom door. It always seemed to linger for days.

I know now that my mother wasn't a bad person, just a victim of her addictions. When she did have spare money, she would put food in the house or buy me clothes from Goodwill. The only pieces of furniture I had in my bedroom was a mattress set and a little blue and white toy chest. Not that I had a lot of toys to put in it, of course, just the three I had gotten for birthdays: one was an art kit, one was a red wagon, and the last, my pride and joy, was a doll named Betsy.

Betsy was my best friend. We would have imaginary tea parties together, sleep together, and even take baths together. Sometimes, I even remember her voice.

When I thought back on my conversations with the doll in adulthood, I realized that I was likely suffering from delusions, thanks to the always present clouds of smoke that laid claim to the dingy hallways and drafty bedrooms of our small apartment.

Still, I remember the sound of her voice: a pleasant, tingling lilt that was almost always coupled with a raucous giggle. I also remember the things that she said to me and the things she wanted me to do. She asked me to steal, usual food or pens and pencils. She wanted me to bring her forks and knives and hit the bad man who slept on our couch. It was always something and I would *always* get in trouble. But she wouldn't. When I told my mother who had put me up to these games she would scoff and shake her head. She never believed me. Adults never do.

Around my 6th birthday I asked my mother for a birthday party. I wanted to invite the mean girls from school and serve them cake and ice cream to make them like me. I remember standing in the kitchen that day with such hopes, having just asked the most important question of my entire life. The glass bottle of coca-cola I held was shaking in my nervous hands. I waited with bated breath as my mother continued putting groceries away, almost as if she hadn't heard me. But I knew she had. Finally, just as I had failed a second time to muster the courage to repeat my question, she turned around and gave me a flippant shake of her head.

"A birthday party? Laura, that's ridiculous, I can't afford to feed 15 children that aren't even mine. Hell, I can barely afford to feed you! You eat like an elephant, especially for a girl your size. Or, I'm sorry, *Betsy* does. There's barely anything left for me to eat around here, much less a classroom of other people's brats."

My face fell as she shook her head, mumbled something else under her breath and stumbled off into the living room. I heard the music go up then as more people walked in the door. Some left, some stayed; I never knew them either way.

It simply wasn't fair, my mother threw parties all the time. What about me? I was a kid! All my friends had birthday parties and now the mean girls at school would know I was too poor to have one and they would tease me even more.

I felt tears start to well in the corners of my eyes and I choked back a sob while I ran to my room and slammed the door behind me. Betsy was lying on the bed and smiling. She was always smiling. Usually it made me feel better but today it just made me angry. She just kept staring at me, smiling. She was going to tell me to do something bad, again. This was why mother wouldn't throw me a birthday party. It was because of all the trouble I got into because of *her*. This was her fault! Betsy didn't have to go to school and Betsy *never* got in trouble like I did. And in my young mind, I truly believed it was the doll, not my mother, who was to blame for everything.

I snapped then. I screamed in indignant rage and I threw the bottle as hard as I could at the bed. It hit Betsy on her forehead and she fell on the floor. Good. I picked up the bottle and I hit her again and again. I thought I heard her laugh and I hit her harder. Then I laughed. When my rage was spent, I dragged Betsy to my toy chest and threw her in. I slammed it shut and kicked the chest against the wall; I never wanted to see Betsy again - ever.

I never owned another doll after Betsy. About a week later the police came and two nice ladies took me to live in a new home in a new state, with food and toys and no drugs. The trunk went into storage and the wagon disappeared. I never saw my mother again. As I got older, my foster parents admitted she was in jail, doing 25 years. That was fine with me; I felt nothing for her anyway. I still had nightmares because of my life with that woman. But then slowly, I began to heal. I focused on doing well in school and I ignored my mother's letters from prison. She reached out to me several times in my 20's, as well, but I always declined her calls.

That is, until this morning. I'm 30 now, with my own children and a loving, honest husband. I have a beautiful house, two dogs and a career as a social worker trying to make a difference for kids who had it bad like me. I'm happy, I'm steady, and I'm content. So when I got a voicemail from my mother informing me she had been paroled and that she wished to speak, decided to let her say her piece.

Since the kids were home from school I went out into our shed in the backyard to return my mother's call. The shed was the children's domain and they used it to play in the summer. I sat on my old toy chest which was currently being used as tea party table and dialed the number she had left me.

Three rings.

"Hello? Laura?"

"Hello, mother. How are you?"

"Oh Laura, thank you for speaking to me. I know you have your own life now and a family. I would love to meet them someday! I just wanted to tell you how sorry I am. For everything."

"Mother, you are not meeting my kids - ever. And since you called me, I am going to what I have needed to say for years. The opium, the heroin, they destroyed you. And the worst of it is that you almost took me down with you. I was five. That was no home for a child. Honestly, I'm surprised it took you so long to get caught."

"Laura, I know how it seems, but I honestly know nothing! Look, it hardly matters and I do understand why you would feel that way. Why you would hate me and not want me to meet your little ones. I learned a lot about forgiveness while I was away and just...oh Laura, I am so sorry about Betsy."

3

"Betsy?" I paused, confused. "Why would you care about her?"

"I know, Laura, believe me I do. It was all my fault, the drugs, the partying. And Betsy, oh God, if I had only paid attention, if I had only known. She's gone and it's because of me."

As my mother began to cry, I tapped my fingers on the toy box, impatiently. The drugs had clearly fried her brain.

"Mother," I sighed. "Why are you talking about Betsy? And why do you even care? I know where Betsy is." *Right underneath me.*

"What are you talking about, Laura? Oh God, where is she?!"

I shifted uncomfortably. "Well...Betsy's in the trunk, where she's always been."

There was a beat of stunning silence.

"What do you mean your sister's in the trunk?"

"Sister? What the hell are you talking about? Back on drugs so soon? That's a record, even for you. Betsy is a goddamn doll. I locked her in my toy box a few days before you got arrested for possession."

"Laura... oh God, no...no... Laura, what have you done? I wasn't arrested because of the drugs, Laura, I was arrested because of Betsy's disappearance! You always called her your little doll, but we thought you knew! Oh God. We thought you knew. Laura, no, what have you done to my baby?!"

My mind had gone blank and with no emotion I set the phone down next to me and stood up. I could hear the muffled sound of my mother's anguished cries and feel the dark clutch of possibility in my own chest. Memories were stirring in the back of my mind, threatening to flood forward into my consciousness. They pushed against a door in my mind that had been locked so tightly for so long that I had forgotten it was even there.

Was it even possible? Could the trauma and the opium have really led me to believe that a small child was actually doll? Begging for food and utensils to eat with, asking me to protect her from the bad man?

No...

I slowly turned around and brought my eyes down the makeshift tea party table. Surely, it was too small; you couldn't fit a person in there. You couldn't. But then, what about a very small, starving, emaciated child? What about her, would she fit? Would an investigator even bother looking for a person in this chest? I knew I wouldn't. It was just too small. And I was sure we had opened the toy box at some point over the years, hadn't we? Or had something swimming in the dark recesses of my memoires always stopped me? I couldn't remember ever seeing it open.

I knelt down to the ground and opened the clasps. It would be better to not look. After all that I had overcome, this new life that I had earned for myself. It could all be undone by opening this toy box. I shouldn't open it. I should throw it in a landfill and forget it ever existed. I should not look inside...

I opened the chest.

I never had a doll. My mother never could afford to buy me one. I never had a wagon either, for that matter. But I did have a toy box; a pretty, blue and white toy box. And when I was five, I beat my little sister to death and put her in it. And now my life is over.

DEATH AT 423 STEERBORN STREET

We've always lived at 423 Steerborn Street, so there really wasn't ever a time that I didn't hear the creature. He'd been living in the room on the other side of my wall since I was born.

When I was a very young child, I thought He was my friend. I would knock and He would bang back. I would giggle and He would mumble words to me that I couldn't understand. I thought He was there to protect me from my nightmares. But as I got older, I started to be afraid. My parents insisted that there wasn't a room on the other side of my wall. Over time, I realized that He wasn't my friend at all. That's when the scratching, moaning and sporadic banging began to scare me.

When I was eight I finally broke down and told my parents about the creature in my wall. I was terrified that He would come into my room one night and kill me. My mother rolled her eyes and told me it was mice. She never listened to me, anyway. My father agreed with her that it was animals, but he hugged me and told me he would protect me and not to be scared.

So from then on whenever I'd hear the noises I would scream for my father and he would come running into my room less than a minute later to see what the matter was. I would point at the wall and cower. My dad would smile, bang on the wall with his fist and say: "Quiet down in there or else!" The noise would stop, I'd give my dad a teary smile and he would hug me. He was always my protector. I miss him so much, now.

As I matured into a teenager I started inviting my friends to sleepover. They didn't believe my stories at first but after one night in my room - they were convinced. We called ourselves the Steerborn Street Ghostbusters and we spent hours trying to exorcise the entity (a demon, according to our research) through awkward séances and Ouija boards. We decided that the scratching must be the creature etching satanic sigils and drawings into the other side of my wall.

One slumber party, running on heightened bravado and caffeine, I waited until the familiar scratching started and I pounded on the wall, just like my dad.

"QUIET DOWN IN THERE OR ELSE. YOU'RE ALREADY DEAD. THE LIVING ARE TRYING TO SLEEP!"

We giggled and my friends were impressed - for a moment. I should have known not to provoke him.

Suddenly there was an answering enraged banging on my wall, louder than I'd ever heard, and a sort of angry yelling. We all screamed and hid in the closet, yelling for my dad. When he came running, my friends begged him to take them home. I was left alone while they were gone. I could feel Him, almost see Him impatiently pacing behind the wall, back and forth, 5 inches of wood and wallpaper between He and I. I was so scared that I stayed hidden in the closet. Then the scratching started again.

That was when I realized what it was doing: it was trying to carve its way through the wall and into my bedroom. I whimpered at the thought and then scratching stopped and the banging resumed on the walls. It didn't stop again until the headlights of my dad's car lit up my room. I cried until my dad, always the hero, came sprinting into my room and banged on the wall.

"It's still in the walls, Dad!" I wailed.

He nodded, gave me a pitying look and pounded his fist on the demon's wall. "Quiet down in there or else!"

Then he held me, let me cry out my fears, and told me it was okay if I slept on the sofa that night. Sometimes I thought he believed it was all in my head. But it wasn't. The murmurs, the knocking, and the scratching, I'd been hearing it all my life. It was real. But if he didn't believe he never let on and never made me feel crazy. He just played along. I guess I never really understood my dad.

One night when I was 16, I was awoken by an otherworldly, ear-splitting scream. It was so loud, so high and so piercing that I screamed as well, in terror. The scream ended abruptly then and a moment later my dad came running in.

"You heard it!" I cried as my body wracked with sobs. "How could you not hear it? You had to have heard it."

"Oh sweetie." My dad sat at the end of my bed, his hair disheveled and a far-off look in his middle-of-the-night, bloodshot eyes. "Of course I heard it, but it was just an owl, I'm sure of it. We've been seeing a few in the neighborhood."

"No dad, listen to the *walls*."

"Lindsey-"

"*Please*, Dad."

He sighed but nodded and we sat and listened for awhile. I needed my dad to know the truth and to finally believe me. We were all in danger.

But no more sounds came from the wall that night.

I didn't hear Him again after that, not for a long time. The wall suddenly felt empty to me for the first time in my life. Maybe it was dormant or maybe it had been called back to Hell. But either way, I knew it would be back.

Oddly, when the creature did return I didn't really notice at first. After 16 years it was simply white noise to me: a background soundtrack as familiar to me as my own face. It took so long for me to process that it was back that I can't put my finger on when it actually started. I think that's what sealed our fates, in the end. The noises were just so inherent to me that I failed to understand how unusual they really were, and had been all along. When I finally *did* realize what I was hearing I'm ashamed to say I felt almost relieved.

The haunt progressed in the same cycle it had all my life. First, the groans, then the banging, then light, lazy tapping, and then, finally, the scratching, always the scratching.

I'd told my dad about the scratching, and about how I thought the creature was trying to rip through the wall and into my room. My dad laughed and told me there were 3 inches of solid metal on the other side of my wall and that nothing; not mice, raccoons, feral cats or even ghosts could come through my wall. And he should know, he'd built the house himself. And besides, he assured me, he would always be there to protect me. But in the end, he wasn't.

Since I was moving out in a year, I decided I had no choice but to just stick it out. After 16 years with Him, what was 12 more months? I grew unconcerned, lazy, and complacent. I ignored the noises, even started to bang back, again. I used logic to pacify my fear: whatever it was, it couldn't come through the wall. If it could, it would've done so years ago. And I sensed that more than anything else in the world, it wanted OUT. And since it was still in there, obviously, it was trapped. And I was right.

The night the door was opened is the most vivid memory I have. I was at a friend's house when my mother called me and told me to come home immediately. This, in itself, was strange as my mother barely even acknowledged me and never, ever called me.

I drove the 5 miles back to my neighborhood but I had a hard time getting in. I started to panic as I desperately weaved through all the media vans, police cars, and SWAT trucks. I had to park and walk the final three blocks to my house, tears rolling down my cheeks as I realized that my street was at the epicenter of it all. Because I knew. As soon as I saw my house, I realized it - my dad must be dead. It had finally gotten out and it had killed my dad.

I took off at a dead run then, ignoring all the voices yelling at me to stop. I dodged in between the vehicles, pushing past dozens of people, ran through the crime scene tape and directly into my house - and there it was. Across from the living room, next to my bedroom, the hall closet stood with its door open. All the jackets and sweaters had been pulled out of it and on the back wall I saw it - another door.

For whatever reason, no one stopped me. I stumbled into the closet, through the hidden door, and out into the room I'd always known was there. But it wasn't what I thought it'd be.

The media called my dad The Skinner of Steerborn Street. And from what I saw in that room, it was a very fitting name. There were knives, all sorts really. And there were metal devices stacked along one wall, at least a hundred of them. Most I didn't recognize, but a few I had seen in history books. There were 4 set of manacles, a wall of chains and rolls of duct tape. In the middle of the room there was a flat table which was, very clearly, blood soaked. A tall stool sat at the head of the table.

But the worst of it was the wall - my wall. Every inch of it was covered in carvings. But the carvings weren't satanic or evil like I'd thought. The carvings were words.

Jacob, I love you. -Diana Hobb

Tell my father I forgive him. -Brian Woodlin

Tara, I'm so sorry. -Michael Mcnulty

Tell my daughters they were my world. -Angela Waterstone

According to the evidence file there were over 60 of these messages. And I made myself read every single one. They haunt me every night. I had spent ten years tormenting them and they would now forever torment me.

I live in a hospital now and I can still hear the scratching. Every time I close my eyes, I hear it. I haven't really slept in a year. My doctor says if I don't sleep soon, I'll die. I spend my days watching news coverage of my father's trial, and I spend my nights staring at the walls. The drugs don't work, but they keep giving them to me anyway. And though I try every night, I can never fall asleep. I always hear the scratching. And I always will.

WHO KILLED JACOB BENNETT?

I live in a backwoods, crappy town in the Midwest. It's a boring, medium sized city carved out of the dense Ozarks of Southeast Missouri. Growing up here had been difficult. I come from a large, violent family and it was no secret that the Cooper kids got beaten. Of course, lots of kids around here get beaten. That's just the kind of town it is.

Since I wasn't allowed to have any friends, I'd concentrated on my grades so that one day I could escape to a 4 year university on the other side of the state. I never thought that after graduating Magna Cum Laude from MSU I would end up back in Harrington, and I might have killed myself if I'd known it.

I often wondered about where I had slipped up along the way. I'd had a bright, exciting future in front of me, far away from Harrington and the drunken, redneck family I'd left behind. But it didn't seem to be any one thing that brought me back. It was just a series of missteps and bad luck. There was no one thing to blame, which made it all the more frustrating.

Teaching English at a community college was a far cry from the literary agent I'd dreamed of being. Every day that I woke up in Harrington felt like a failure. The only thing I enjoyed about the town was the crisp nature that surrounded it. My small home backed right up to the Ozarks and every weekend I went hiking in the woods to clear my mind; always taking the same path by the river and always coming home refreshed and content. I considered them my mini-vacations and they kept me sane.

But it was this very practice of mine that lead to the single most horrific moment of my life. It could have been anyone in town who'd found her - hundreds of people go out into those woods- but it wasn't just anyone, it was me.

I don't know what came over me that Sunday, but for some reason I didn't want to hike my usual trail. Maybe it was the difficult week I'd had, or the fact that my hand was feeling so very stiff (I'd broken it years before) or perhaps it was because my creepy stalker had been dancing on the fringes of his 100 yard legal restriction all week. Or maybe it was everything combined. For whatever reason, I decided on a change in my routine that day.

Since I had brought my GPS I decided to let my thoughts and body drift where they may. I wandered lazily and mindlessly, letting the fresh, cool air purify my soul, as it always did. I thought about the exam I was giving the following week. I thought about taking my dog Clara to puppy training classes. I thought about calling in another complaint about Doug the Stalker. I thought about everything for awhile and then I thought about nothing.

After about an hour I realized that I had stumbled onto a narrow, barely visible trail. The crisp, thin morning air was slowly giving way to its warmer, heavier brother. I decided to follow the trail for a quarter mile or so and then turn around and head back. According to my GPS, I was only about 2 miles from home, which wasn't that far at all.

I lost the trail twice, but was able to pick it up again after a few moments both times. Just as I lost the trail for a third time, the tree line broke and I was suddenly standing in a small clearing. I could tell immediately that there was something not right about this place, something ailing. The grass was yellowed and dead and an old, gnarled Burr Oak tree sat in the middle of the glade under thin, weak sunlight.

This place was Creeps-town. I took out my phone and snapped a few photos hoping to somehow capture the eerie aura of the clearing. I walked around the burr oak, stepping over thick, low-hanging branches. I raised my camera to take another photo when something that shouldn't be caught my eye. There was color between the leaves that had no place in the sickly yellows and sullen browns. It was a blue shoe.

I walked closer, curious, and wondering if maybe kids used this place to smoke weed or drink. But when I got closer, I saw the shoe was far too small for a teenager. It was the shoe of a young child - and there was a young child still in the shoe.

I've felt many horrible things in my life - failure, disappointment, pain - but I have never felt anything so horrible as I did when finding the bones of a small child shoved into the alcove of a tree. He was curled up in the fetal position, his broken body much too large for the tiny little alcove. It was a wonder that he had fit there at all when he was more than just bones. His clothes were mostly gone, at least on the exposed side, and his skull had cracks and angry indentations. I vomited on the trunk of the tree and then I'm ashamed to say - I ran.

I ran all 2 miles home, the need to share the burden of this knowledge with someone, anyone, was urgent in me to the point of hysteria. When I finally broke the tree line into my own backyard I fell onto the grass in exhaustion. I stared up at sun, trying to blind myself of the memory. But I could still see that broken little body.

When I could breathe again, I took my phone from my pocket and dialed the police. They came within minutes and I somehow found the strength to stand and meet them in the driveway. I explained everything that had happened in short, choked sentences and handed them my GPS to show them where the body was.

An officer wrapped a blanket around me and another brought me bottles of water. After that, everything happened pretty quickly. I sat in my kitchen and watched out the window as crowds gathered and media arrived. The sound of helicopters came and went from overhead, both police and news choppers alike, I'm sure. I stared out the window shade, praying that the crowds couldn't see me inside.

As dusk began to settle, I found Doug in the gathered crowd of news correspondents and neighbors. He was at the very front of the police tape and he watched both the spectacle and my window, evenly. It was the first time he had ever actually broken the restraining order. I tried to find an officer but I found my bed instead.

The long, emotional day gave way to a deep and sound sleep. When I awoke the next morning, I saw that media vans from St. Louis had arrived and that the cops had set up roadblocks on my street. I called into work that day and the next and finally I told them I wouldn't be coming in the rest of the week. I stayed home and worked on my novel, trying to ignore the circus our town had become.

Identifying the little boy took almost two weeks but the media was using the name "Jacob". I saw the headline "Who put Jacob in the Burr Oak tree?" land on my front porch one day. It

15

seemed the media was drawing comparisons between our case and the case of *Who put Bella in the Wych Elm?* I never retrieved the paper.

Finally, the coroner's office released a statement that the five year old boy had been identified - name withheld while they notified the family - and that the likely, though not conclusive, cause of death was blunt force trauma.

Two days later I was asked to come in and give a recorded, official statement to the lead detective on the case. I went over everything I could remember from that day in extreme detail, even seeing Doug in the gathering crowd. The detective nodded his head throughout my testament and then, when I was finished, pressed stop on the recorder and left the room.

I drummed my fingers on the table and absentmindedly stared up at the camera in the corner until he returned ten minutes later.

The door opened and the lead detective walked back into the room with a stranger in tow. He was tall, tanned, and sported slicked back white hair. I instantly disliked him.

"Ms. Cooper, this is Dr. Watner. Do you remember Dr. Watner?"

"No. Should I?"

"Not necessarily." The doctor replied.

"Why am I still here?"

"Because of Jacob." The detective sat down across from me.

"Is Jacob the boy in the tree?"

"Jacob is your son." The doctor answered.

"I don't have a son." I said shaking my head.

"Jessica," the doctor began, "we met several years ago when your son first disappeared. You blamed a man named Doug Ozinga for taking him, you were hysterical about it. Do you remember that?"

"I know Doug Ozinga; I have a restraining order against him. But that's where my part in this ends, I don't have a son." I repeated, slowly.

"Jessica, I'm going to show you some pictures now that might upset you."

The doctor spread three large photos out in front of me. As soon as I saw their content my hands began to shake. But I wasn't afraid. I was confused.

"I don't remember these pictures. I don't know who that is."

The photos were of me with a young, blonde boy of about four. We were both smiling and hugging.

"Do you agree that the person in this picture is you?"

I continued to stare at the photos. There was no denying it; I still had some of the clothes I was wearing in the photo.

"Yes."

"And does the child in this picture look at all familiar to you?"

The answer was no - and yes. He was a stranger but I felt like he was stranger who I'd seen somewhere before. Memories began to tug at the tips of my synapses but they were hazy and clouded.

"Yes." I murmured, my eyes never leaving the page.

The detective leaned forward in his chair. "I'm so sorry, Jessica. The body that was in the tree has been identified as your son Jacob."

"What..." I was lost, and suddenly feeling terribly alone. "What do I do?"

"I think you should take some more time talking to Dr. Watner, you're going to need support now."

"I still don't believe it, but what about the little boy? I saw Doug Ozinga on the day the body was found, he was at the crime scene!"

"Yes, I expected that."

The detective stood up then, and Dr. Watner followed.

"We will return shortly. Would you like me to call your family?"

But I had no family.

"No," I said quietly.

"I understand," the detective said as he followed Dr Watner through the door.

"Wait!" I yelled suddenly, rising from my chair. The detective stopped and turned around. "When are you going to arrest Doug Ozinga? Do you have any evidence on him yet?"

"Jessica...Doug Ozinga doesn't exist. He never has."

He closed the door behind him and I fell back into my chair. It's been almost two hours and they haven't come back. And it makes me wonder why I'm still here.

But I think I know. My 6 year old son disappeared. Doug Ozinga doesn't exist. And I found a body in the woods.

PARADISE PINE

About five years ago my husband and I decided to spend Thanksgiving at a cabin up north. We planned on starting a family the following year and so we wanted one last romantic holiday with just the two of us. We found the place online through a website we've used in the past and booked it for a week. The cabin was located outside of Pinetop, Arizona and the owner warned us that it can be hard to get back to in the winter because of the snow. The property was 13 miles from the nearest town and 4 miles from the nearest paved road. Aaron and I weren't worried, however, since our jeep had snow tires and we were also bringing tire chains.

We arrived on a Friday afternoon. We had made excellent time on the drive as there was actually very little snow on the ground. We decided to take a tour of the cabin before we unloaded the car. The cabin, named Paradise Pine, was three stories tall and built into the side of a mountain. The top floor was simply the master bedroom, which was connected to a second story patio-balcony via a sliding glass door. The front door was located on the ground floor, along with the kitchen and living room, and the basement housed a washer, a dryer and a wood furnace that heated the cabin through a large pipe that extended up through all three floors.

Even though the views through the bay windows were beautiful, the first thing we noticed when we walked in was that the cabin hadn't been cleaned. Often times with very rural properties, the owner will offer to waive the $150 cleaning fee if you are willing to clean the place yourself before you depart. Most guests opt to do this, but in the rare occurrence they don't, the owner sends a cleaning crew. The previous tenants in this cabin had clearly decided not to clean, and also not to inform the owner that they were leaving it dirty. Since it was a holiday and a snowstorm was forecasted for early next week, we decided to clean the cabin ourselves and ask the owner to reduce our bill when we left the following Friday. We brought everything in from the jeep and got to work with dishes and laundry. Afterwards, we made an easy dinner, opened a bottle of wine, and played a few games of billiards on the pool table in the living room.

The temperature started to plummet at around six in the evening and I asked my husband, Aaron, to go down and light the furnace in the basement. I went up to the bedroom to wash my face and change into warmer clothes. The bathroom connected to our bedroom was oddly door-less, had a broken mirror and a torn-down shower curtain. *Wow, there've been some cowboys in here.* They hadn't even bothered to pick the glass up off the floor before they left. I did so carefully, regretting the stupidity of the drunken idiots who must have stayed here the week before. I took a few photos with my phone and planned to send them to the owner when we got back to town on Monday. I certainly didn't want to be charged for damage inflicted by the previous tenants.

I met Aaron on the ground level and told him about the bathroom.

"Well, that's not the only thing that's broken. The light's out in the basement and I couldn't find a flashlight. I did manage to find the furnace though. I squirted some of that cheap vodka your sister sent in there, threw in a match and hoped for the best."

"Seems to be working," I stammered through now chattering teeth, "I can feel the heat coming through." I held my hands up to the metal pipe that wound its way around the house. "Keep the basement door closed. It's freezing down there."

One of our favorite things to do when staying at a cabin is to read through all the journal entries of the previous guests. Usually, it was just things like "Went fishing with the kids, caught a bass" or "had a BBQ, played cards with the family", but occasionally you found something more interesting, like "got drunk, set a tree on fire."

We found the Paradise Pine diary and snuggled up on the couch. Aaron read aloud the first four or five entries before I decided to take over. We were about halfway through the book when we called it a night and went to bed.

The following evening we stayed up late as we had had a long nap that day. The plan had been to go on a hike but it had been too cold out. Luckily, the furnace in the basement was, to our amazement, still burning. We spent the whole day lazing around the living room. After dinner, Aaron practiced pool while I read aloud from the journal, starting where we had left off. I read for an hour before finally arriving at the journal entry of the guests who had stayed before us. I was very interested in this one; these people had to have a good story. The writer had chosen to format his entries into dates with time stamps. There were over 6 pages and I could already tell the handwriting sort of disintegrated as the days wore on.

"Wow, they must have been drunk ALL weekend, look at how messy this handwriting gets!" I held the book up to Aaron.

"Can you read it?" He asked, spinning the 8 ball into a corner pocket.

"Of course! I'm great at reading other people's shitty handwriting by now." I sent him an impish grin and took another sip of wine before beginning to read.

Sunday, Nov 4th 3:30PM

Wow, what a beautiful cabin! My wife and I booked this place for two weeks on a whim and we can't believe how lucky we got! Barely made it back here with the truck, there's snow everywhere. At least a foot deep. And it's below 40 degrees outside – thankfully the furnace in the basement is HUGE, as promised by Marissa, so all three floors are warm and cozy!

Monday, Nov 5th 11:30AM

We're snowed in! We had wanted to run home today to grab a few things we forgot but that is definitely not happening. The road is unmanageable so it appears we aren't going anywhere. Looks like we will be spending most of our

21

day inside, drinking mimosas and playing poker. As you can see, we aren't too upset about it!

Tuesday, Nov 6th 7:25PM

My wife Sarah is currently cooking up a delicious roast chicken and I'm finally going to start writing. This is the reason we came here, after all, and I refuse waste the opportunity to cure my writer's block. It's just so gorgeous here I haven't written a damn thing! I also saw someone walking around the tree line today. I have no idea how they are surviving out there, we won't even go outside! It was 34 degrees last I checked.

Wednesday Nov 7th 9PM

Today Sarah and I made a snow man and snow angels! We don't get snow in Scottsdale, so we are taking full advantage of it. I haven't been able to write anything new, but I did edit the previous two chapters of my book. I think the beauty of this place is just too distracting. I'm kidding! (Sort of).

I think we may have neighbors. I was having a cigarette out on the balcony last night and I saw someone at the tree line again. He is extremely tall. And certainly close enough to say hello but when I waved he walked back into the woods. Will have to ask Marissa about this? She didn't mention any neighbors nearby.

Thursday Nov 8th 1PM

This morning I woke up to find animal tracks all around the outside of the cabin. I don't know what sort of animal made them. The prints were the shape of a rectangle, almost like they were made by the end of a 2x4. By the time Sarah got up at 11, the snow had mostly melted but you could still kind of see them. I think last night's snow is the last we will get while we are here. The sky is looking pretty clear. Sarah thinks I am succumbing to cabin fever, so today we are going for a hike since it's so beautiful out.

Friday Nov 9th 7AM

Last night someone tried to get into the house. I woke up at about 1 in the morning to the sound of banging on the front door. Not knocking, banging. I went downstairs and grabbed a pool stick. I asked who it was and the banging stopped. I waited a few minutes and then opened the door but there was nothing there. I started back up the stairs to wake up Sarah, as she is a heavy sleeper. The banging sounded again, more urgently this time, and from the other side of the room, on the wall next to the bookshelf. It stopped after a long minute and I sat down on the steps and waited all night for them to try something. Nothing happened after that.

Friday Nov 9th 2PM

I told Sarah what happened and she wants to leave. I'm not really convinced, but Sarah scares easily. I will admit that I'm a bit on edge. I tried to start the car this morning but nothing happened. I'm not a car guy and I have no idea what to do. We can't hike out, there's no signal out here and we can't find a house phone. We talked about it and decided we're just going wait it out here. I know people have this cabin rented out on the 16th so we'll just have to wait the week for them. I did find a wood axe which I'm keeping in the bedroom, just in case they come back to harass us. I think it's probably a homeless person living out in the woods. There were tracks around the house again this morning and I'm no longer convinced they're from an animal. We'll see if they come back.

Saturday 5AM

Last night the knocking was back. But it was something knocking on the sliding door to our bedroom – from the second story patio. I don't know how it climbed up there. It knocked on the window, gently, almost coaxingly. A thin curtain covers the sliding glass door so I couldn't see what it was. The knocking finally stopped and a full minute later it started again, becoming the loud, insistent banging of the night before. I reached over Sarah and grabbed the axe, bounding out of bed as she screamed. By the time I got to the sliding door the *banging has stopped. I threw back the curtain but there was no one on the patio. In the moonlight, I saw it walking away from the cabin, back toward the tree line. Sarah stumbled over to the window and I showed her the retreating figure. She covered her face and cried. What we saw terrified us both.*

It's not a human. It's tall, maybe 10 feet, and skinny. It looks like a black stick figure, impossibly thin. It has no hands or feet just stumps. And no face. It's just a black oval, with no features. The contrast was horrifying, this tall, black stick man walking through the snow. It reached the tree line and disappeared. I spent the next hour trying to calm Sarah down. She said we need to leave. I think she's right. When we were finally calm enough to lie in bed again, the silence was deafening. I felt myself slowly start to drift off. It was out of this silence that the knocking came again – this time on our bedroom door. I jumped out of bed and grabbed the axe again. Sarah backed into a corner and screamed. By the time I threw open the door the knocking had stopped and there was nothing there, but the front door was wide open. It can get inside the cabin. I don't know what it wants.

Saturday 5PM

I am terrified. My wife is terrified. Today I considered setting the car on fire, just to see if the smoke would attract someone's attention. Sarah wouldn't let me because it's our only way out. So we packed the car up instead. Maybe when the snow melts more, we'll be able to fix the car. I catch Sarah staring off a lot and she hasn't said much since she saw the stick man. Seeing the thing, it's affected me too. I have been having migraines today. I've never had a migraine before. I want to protect my wife but I don't know what to do. I caught Sarah staring at me, almost in a trance earlier. I asked her what was wrong and she said "It eats us." She seemed to snap out of it pretty quick after that and asked me why I was staring at her. She doesn't remember saying it and we can't figure out what it means. This thing is fucking with our heads.

Sunday 10AM

Last night I stayed up all night. It's lightly snowing. All was quiet.

Sunday 7PM

I found footprints this afternoon on the upstairs balcony. The same rectangle ones the stick man makes. He was outside our window again. I brushed them away before Sarah could see. It stopped snowing an hour ago and its twilight now. I can see him in the tree line. I saw him turn around and walk back into the woods. His profile is as thin as a piece of paper. The stick man came back, though. I think we're going to die here.

Monday Nov 12th 9AM

Last night I went out on the balcony at around 8 for a cigarette. I heard a noise behind me and turned to see the stick man on the roof, 5 feet above me. I ran back inside to grab the axe and screamed at Sarah to arm herself. I turned around to run back outside and heard the stick man running above me on the roof, in the same direction. When I got outside, the thing was gone. I saw it running off into the trees again. But it was different. It was taller. I think there's more than one. When I got back inside, Sarah had locked herself in the upstairs bathroom. She was hysterical and kept saying she was going to die here. I tried to give her the pool stick but she wouldn't open the door for anything. I sat on the bed and waited. At some point Sarah must have fallen asleep because all was quiet. It was then that I first heard it walking around in the kitchen. I backed away from the bedroom door, courage suddenly failing me. It was in the house. I waited for more sounds from the kitchen but none came. After a few minutes, I finally heard a thump. It was on the stairs. It was climbing the stairs.

Thump. Slowly, but loudly. Thump. I banged the bedroom door from my side and told it to leave us alone. Thump. Sarah was screaming again, sobbing. It could hurt me, but I would never let it hurt my family. It stopped when it got to the top step. I could feel it on the other side of the door. It didn't make a noise. I tried to think of a strategy that would give me the upper hand if it attacked. I finally decided that if I threw the door open, it would knock the stick man down the stairs. On the count of three I turned the handle and kicked the door. It swung open freely, and I saw the black stick man still down on the landing of the stairs, facing me. It was more than 10 feet tall. I was paralyzed with horror for several long seconds when it started running up the stairs at me without warning. I stumbled back into the room as fast as I could as I realized that death at the hands of the stick man was more than death. Worse than death. It ate you. It kept you.

It stopped at the top step and dipped it head through the door taking 2 steps into the room. It was just a tall black shadow. Almost more of a dense absence of light than a solid black. Realizing the axe was still in my hand I moved between the stick man and the bathroom door. I raised the axe to attack, and at that moment the stick man screamed. It was unlike anything I had ever heard before. I wanted to hold my hands over my ears as I felt an ebbing thunder in my brain. I heard the mirror shatter in the bathroom from the sound. I thought of Sarah. With the last ounce of strength I had I ran at the thing, axe high and brought it down in the creature's chest. Over and over again for what felt like forever but was probably no time at all. It threw me aside and I heard my wife scream. That's the last thing I remember before I passed out.

When I opened my eyes again it was mid-morning. My wife was gone. The bathroom door was gone. And the axe was gone. I looked for Sarah all morning; I walked deep into the woods. I searched for miles. I am going to sleep for a few minutes and then go back out into the woods to find her. I hope I meet the stick man. If Sarah is dead, I want to be dead too. I think that's what it wanted all along.

Monday Nov 12th 6PM

It's getting dark and harder to search the woods. In my mind, all I hear is her voice. It eats us. Over and over again. What has it done to her?

I couldn't save her. After everything, I couldn't save her. When I first realized I had forgotten my medication, the snowstorm stopped us from leaving. But when I saw the stick man I thought it had been a blessing in disguise. I needed to be clear-minded and alert to protect my family, and I couldn't do that when I was on the Haloperidol. But it didn't matter in the end anyway. I couldn't save her.

The car started on the first try this morning. It's letting me leave. I'm going to drive around to the other side of the mountain and walk back towards the cabin. Maybe I'll find the stream. Maybe I'll find Sarah. It would be useless to stay another day, the stick man is gone. I know it in my heart. And it's below freezing and the furnace has burned out, the firewood is gone. If I find her I'll come back and let you know. This humble little book is my only friend now.

Aaron had stopped playing pool long ago and the wine hadn't been touched since I started reading. We stared at each other as the last line echoed around the cabin. We both seemed to wake from our paralyzed state at the same time. I threw the book across the room and Aaron backed up into the bookcase saying "Jesus!"

"This is fake, right?" I asked as I stood up. I didn't need the glass of wine anymore. I needed the bottle.

"I don't know, Liv, I don't…I don't think so."

"The guy said he was a writer," I insisted, "He probably just wanted to write a scary story for other guests. Although he really crossed the line into downright disturbing." I took a sip of wine and turned around to see Aaron eyeing the stairs, warily.

"You can't be serious, Aaron. It's creepy as shit, I agree, but come on."

Almost like he didn't hear me, Aaron started ascending the stairs. I don't know what he wanted to see up there, but I put the wine down and followed suit. By the time I got into the bedroom Aaron was sliding the glass door open. I followed him out onto the balcony. You could see the tree line from the patio very clearly. I searched the woods for any movement but saw nothing. I turned to say something to Aaron and found him studying the roof. He threw a wild look at me and walked back inside. I followed him in.

Aaron paced around the room.

"What?!" I was starting to get annoyed.

"It's all just like in the story. You can see the tree line, the field and the roof from the balcony. And look-"

He pointed to the attached bathroom.

"-there are hinges but no door. There should be a door, it's a bathroom. And the mirror-"

"What?" I interjected. "Was shattered by the stick man's scream?!" He was starting to scare me. Aaron was usually the most logical person I knew.

"The stick man? Did you even pay attention to what you read? There was no stick man."

"No shit."

"No, I mean, there never was. His last entry, about the medication - and how they got snowed in and couldn't go back for it – Haloperidol, it's used to treat schizophrenia. Olivia, go read it again. The entire thing is him slowly succumbing to his psychosis, page by page. Hell, his wife knew it was happening!"

"This is madness, Aaron." I walked into the bathroom and looked around. "You think someone died in here? Four days ago?"

Aaron shook his head. "I don't know. I think it's a possibility. The shower curtain is torn down, the mirror is broken. It certainly looks like there could have been a struggle in here. And the door...the axe....both missing."

The logic of his conclusions began to dawn on me.

"Oh my God, if this is real... Aaron, we cleaned this place top to bottom when we got here. If there was a murder, we've destroyed all the evidence!"

"We didn't know. We didn't know that someone died here-"

"We still don't know. Aaron, where's the body?"

"I don't know. Maybe it's buried out in the woods."

"We need to leave; we need to go get help. Let's take the book to the police and tell them what we found when we got here. Just to be safe."

"Okay. Okay, Jesus, this guy could come back anytime. Let's get out of here."

We had just started down the stairs when another thought occurred to me. I stopped on the landing.

"Aaron…"

He turned around, "Yeah?"

"He said the fire in the furnace had burned out. Did you put firewood in when you lit it?"

"No…it was almost pitch black. I couldn't see any firewood."

"But…We've been burning that furnace for almost a day."

I could see the implication slowly dawning over Aaron's face.

"What have we been burning, Aaron?"

He ran for the basement door, and I followed. When he opened the door, I can't describe to you what came up from below. It was a hot, pungent, heavy air. I stood on the top step as Aaron descended into the basement.

"The axe is down here."

I took a deep breath and followed him down. I stopped on the bottom stair, refusing to go any further. It was still very dark but for the light coming down the stairs and a soft orange glow in the back of the room. Aaron knelt in front of the stove door. He looked over at me and I nodded. Aaron slowly turned the handle and pulled open the furnace door. The fire inside lit his face and after moment, the horror expressed there told me everything I needed to know.

***

They found Jason Harding less than a day later. He had hung himself out in the woods, less than 100 yards from the cabin. In fact, he had been hanging there when we pulled up on Sunday, the 18th of November. I've often wondered if he hung himself because he wanted to be with his wife, or if he hung himself because he realized what he had done.

I hoped it was the latter because I hated him so much. Not for his mental illness, not for his crime – but for what he did to us. Sarah Harding had burned in that furnace for a day, and for a day, we had breathed in every atom of her body. We had kept warm by the flesh of her corpse. Why didn't it smell? We were given a very scientific explanation citing high burning temperatures, years of pine infusion, and the pieces of wooden door burning in there with her. But it didn't stop the nightmares.

The case made headline news in the Southwest. Aaron and I managed to prevent our names being associated with Paradise Pine through an anonymity clause on our witness statements. We never told our friends or families we were involved. We tried to forget.

Paradise Pine still stands today. It is available for rent, although the name has been changed. The owner insisted on keeping the cabin journal, so the police tore out Jason Harding's pages and gave it back to her. It still sits on the table next to the bookshelf, and tenants still read it and write in their own experiences.

I pity those people. They will wonder about the torn pages and never learn what was written on them. They will cringe at the door-less bathroom and never know someone was murdered there. They will light the basement furnace and never realize its dark history.

And they will never know that the quiet, charming, peaceful cabin they're staying in…is actually the Paradise Pine.

JUNE 10TH, 1999

When I was a kid I lived in a beautiful house. My mother and my older sister were artists; they painted, sculpted and danced their way through life, challenging and inspiring each other. They created and scrapped works of art in a constant rotation. Our house was forever changing and evolving into something new like it had an organic, vibrant life of its own.

My memories of those days and that house are so very vivid.

Our family room was usually some shade of orange (my sister had painted it for me - orange was my favorite color).

We had a marble bird-shaped fountain in the middle of the kitchen (which I used to splash my mom and sister),

There was a sculpture of a small dancing man on our landing (which I always high-fived),

And of course, the hallway that was painted floor-to-ceiling with fish (which I always laid on the floor to "swim" through).

And, finally, my favorite thing of all, a staircase that my sister had painted like piano keys (although I'm pretty sure it's only because she was in love with her piano teacher).

In short, my house was a magical place that the neighborhood kids couldn't stay away from. Suffice it to say I had a lot of friends.

Since we had the most exciting house in the county, people would always ask to come over and visit. My parents threw countless BBQs, dinner parties, open houses; just give them something to celebrate and they'd throw a party.

I had so many wonderful memories of my life from before the night Anna died. I had so few of the night that it happened. And, perhaps worst of all, I had no memory of the only moment that really mattered. Until I did.

My father owned a locksmith company with my Uncle Peter and they were out on call that night. I think mom was home in her room but I can't quite remember. She was gone a lot in those days. It wasn't until I was older that I learned there were whispers of an affair between my mother and Samuel, the curator of a local art gallery. But that night I'm sure I remember piano music coming from her room. Anna was in bed because she had an early meeting at the gallery to unveil her newest canvas. And I was in my room as usual playing Tomb Raider on my Playstation.

At some point in the night I think I must have heard a noise because I remember pausing my game and cracking my door to look out into the hallway. I recall staring down the corridor toward the staircase trying to adjust my eyes to the dark. I thought there may be someone there so I came out fully into the hallway to see. I remember that for some reason I was afraid to turn on the light so I squinted down the hallway .

There was someone staring back at me. Someone in the dark, someone who had just come up the stairs, someone...I recognized. He stayed completely still, perhaps wondering if I could see him too.

As he stared at me I began feel scared. I wanted to run toward the light-switch but I didn't have the courage. And then, suddenly, in a single breath the figure was moving, sprinting down the hallway toward me. Too afraid to scream, I fell over backward and scrambled into my room as I watched the figure run into Anna's bedroom. I don't remember anything else from that night. Not screaming from Anna's room. Not hiding under the bed. Not falling asleep.

Uncle Peter and my dad had come home together that night after finishing their call. They spent the night drinking in the garage, which was the only room my mother never touched (and the only room my father could relax in). So it was Uncle Peter that found Anna the next morning. She had been beaten to death; her head was completely caved in. I wish I didn't know that but adults talk loudly when they're upset.

I spent the day hiding under my bed, plugging my ears and crying.

My mom was hysterical; screaming and crying so loudly that an ambulance came to take her to the hospital. My father, not knowing what else to do, sent me to stay with Uncle Peter and Aunt Lydia for awhile. It was only a day later that the police showed up at my uncle's door and asked to talk to me.

They sat me down in the living room and my aunt brought me a glass of chocolate milk. They asked me if I had seen anything that night and I told them I had. They asked me what happened and I told them what I knew. They asked me who it was that I'd seen in the hallway and I faltered.

I couldn't remember.

They kept at me until I cried. It felt like hours. My uncle stood in the doorway watching as the detectives asked me the same questions over and over again. Was he tall? Short? Did he have long hair? Was he old or young? What was he wearing? But try as I might, I simply couldn't remember anything. All I knew was that I recognized him. The detectives tried to hide their frustration and anger but ultimately failed. At one point I was so scared of them I thought of making something up. But I didn't want to send anyone I knew to jail.

My parents didn't talk to me at the funeral and it was clear to me that they'd heard about my failure to identify Anna's killer. David the piano teacher talked to me, though, and he cried. I guess he'd had a crush on Anna, too. Most of mother's art friends came over with a few kind words to say. My teacher was there. Samuel the curator didn't come at all.

A few days after the funeral, a child psychologist came to my uncle's house. She asked me the same questions the police did, but in a much gentler way. She didn't get mad at me when I didn't know the answers, either. I heard her tell my aunt and uncle that I had repressed the memory of what I saw and that it happens sometimes when a child is involved in a traumatic event. Uncle Peter asked if I would ever remember who it was. The psychologist said that one day something may trigger it again, but not to pressure me. My uncle nodded, gravely.

A week after that I was sent back home. Or at least, sent somewhere that used to be home. The walls of my house were now all white or gray. The bird fountain was gone, the undersea hallway was gone, the sculpture was gone. Anna's piano stairs were now covered in dark brown carpet. I found my mom drinking a glass of wine and painting over the stars on the floor of the entryway. She didn't look at me for another week. She didn't speak to me for a month.

My once bright, lively home was now the color of Anna's tombstone. I was left alone in my room most of the time. Occasionally my mother would come by and ask matter-of-factly if I remembered yet who it was that had murdered her baby girl. But I hadn't. The asking turned to pressing, the pressing to demanding and the demanding, finally, to hysteria. My father had to stop her from shaking me and screaming at me several times but I didn't mind it. They were the only interactions I had with my mom, anymore.

Once in a while a detective would come by to talk to me but I never had anything new to tell them. My mother took me to a renowned hypnotist behind my father's back and I woke up screaming in hysterics. To my mother's disappointment I hadn't said anything during the session and didn't remember what I'd seen while I was under. My dad was pissed when he found out.

I really did try very hard to remember. I lay in bed every night for four years squeezing my eyes shut and screaming at my brain to show me what my eyes had seen. But it was no use. The memory was there, I could still see the figure in the darkness. But it had no face.

And because I *knew* that the person I'd seen that night was someone I knew, someone who was probably still around, I was constantly afraid. I hid from my uncle, Samuel, my mother's art friends, even my dad.

But worse then all of that was just knowing that I'd failed Anna. I fell asleep in tears more nights than not.

Eventually I was old enough to go away to college. I stopped crying at night and started drinking instead. It came to a point where I couldn't fall asleep unless I was blackout drunk. I no longer wanted to remember what I'd seen. It had been too many years; the wounds were old and finally starting to heal. I didn't need to know the truth of what happened that night and I convinced myself it didn't matter anymore, anyway.

As graduation neared I was surprised to hear from my dad that my mother was planning to attend the ceremony. I spent all of my summers and holidays on campus and I hadn't spoken to her in four years. I was hesitant didn't know what to expect.

When the day came, I nervously waited for my parents' car to pull up outside of my apartment. As soon as she got out of the car, my mom threw her arms around me and cried. She apologized for abandoning me when I needed her most and she begged my forgiveness. I hugged her back and told her how much I'd missed her. It had taken 18 years, but my mom was finally getting better and it was the happiest day of my life. My parents asked me to come home after graduation and live in my old room while I looked for a job. As any broke, homeless, new graduate would, I excitedly agreed.

I drove home on a Friday and found a surprise graduation party waiting for me when I arrived. And that wasn't even the best part. The best part was that my house was no longer shades of gray and death- it was a menagerie of color and life again. Life that had been breathed back into my childhood home, even dad didn't seem to mind it anymore. The fountain, the fish hallway, they were all back!

I spent the night laughing and clinking glasses with people I hadn't seen since the funeral. David the piano teacher was there, married now, with his youngest son. Uncle Peter shook my hand and told me I'd become a fine young man. Aunt Lydia hugged me tightly. Some of mother's art friends were there, too, and they hadn't changed at all- they still talked loudly and often.

Close to midnight, though the party was in full swing, I decided I needed a break to just quietly appreciate how life could take you to rock bottom and then raise you back up in such eloquent ways. I wandered around the house, quietly admiring some of my mother's new pieces.

I made it upstairs and found that my room had been converted into a more respectable, adult bedroom with a flat screen and a computer desk. And I was happy to see they'd left me my PS1! I peaked into my parent's bedroom, too, and admired the Saharan theme before walking down the hall to come face to face with the very last bedroom - Anna's. I leaned my head against the closed door for a few moments and sighed deeply.

35

"I'm sorry, Anna," I whispered before pushing the door in.

Anna's room was a mausoleum. It looked exactly as it had the night she'd died only the bed was made with different linens and the carpet had been replaced. All the blood covered up or cleaned away. I couldn't bring myself to go in.

I suddenly heard a wooden creak on my right and snapped my head toward the staircase. A man was coming up the stairs and he had paused on the landing to lean against the dancing man statue and turned to smile at me. My glass fell to the floor to shatter at my feet.

You'd think a repressed memory would come back to you slowly, ebbing and flowing like a wave on a beach, leaving behind tendrils of the truth with each swell. But it wasn't like that at all. As soon as I saw his face, I knew, and I remembered everything.

The dancing man stared up at me from beside the stranger on the landing. And even though it hadn't moved, I could feel it staring back at me.

The panic began to well in my chest just as they did all those years ago, when the dancing man had climbed the stairs to stare at me in the darkness. I remember it all now. I remember, too, Anna's screams when the statue entered her room. I remember my mother's piano gently playing Vivaldi over the sounds of my sister's bones cracking and her flesh tearing.

I remember when the dancing man, covered in blood, appeared at my door and danced to my mother's music, his smile growing bigger and toothier every second. And I remember when he danced away, leaving a dark trail of my sister's blood behind him. I remember everything now.

THE DISAPPEARANCE OF EMILY MORGAN

It's funny what you remember as a kid. I don't remember my 5th birthday or my first day of school. But I remember very clearly the day my dog died. It's been 12 years now, and it's still the most vivid memory of my childhood.

My sister Emily and I were typical twins. Always hatching diabolical plans and getting into trouble together. On this particular day, we had colored our cat, Pongo, blue. Even though my mom tried to punish us separately - me on the stairs, Emily in the dining room - we were still making faces at each other and giggling. She was just about to scold us when the doorbell rang.

My mother gave us both a you-better-not-move-a-muscle look as she went to answer the door.

Standing on our stoop was a tall, lanky blonde man wearing a red tracksuit. I remember he had shifting, watery eyes. He noticed Emily and me immediately.

What *we* noticed was that he was holding our dog, Rocky under one arm like a sack of flour. Emily called to Rocky softly, but the dog didn't move. The man began to talk lowly with my mother. She cupped a hand over her mouth and I heard him say "Do you mind if I use your hose?"

My mother rushed us upstairs to our room and we watched out the window as the man rinsed off his fender in front of our house. It was our first taste of death and we cried for two days. We were six.

My parents, deciding to use the sad occasion as an opportunity to teach us about death, held a funeral in our backyard for Rocky. Emily and I cried as we read a poem we had written together the night before.

My mother held us as my father hammered a white, wooden cross into the ground bearing Rocky's name. Even our older brother Eric was there, which was nice because he was almost always next door playing video games and smoking something smelly with the neighbor kids. I think I saw him tear up a little. We had loved Rocky.

That was only two months before it happened.

What I remember much less clearly was the night that Emily disappeared.

My parents had thrown a going away party for Eric, who was leaving for a semester abroad in Japan. Emily and I had begged them to make it a pool party and we'd finally worn them down after much pestering. The pool had only gone in three months before and it was our official christening party!

Oddly, I remember only bits and pieces of that night. My father was drunk. My mother was giving tours of our newly remodeled house to everyone, whether they wanted to see it or not. My brother was in the living room with his friends playing video games. And Emily and I were in the pool playing mermaids, which was our favorite game.

My uncle Cliff gave us rubber bands which we used to bind our ankles together. We then swam around the pool pretending to be mermaid princesses. Just after it got dark my mom called us for dinner. We both jumped out of the pool and ran around the edge before my father yelled at us.

"Rachel! Emily! No running or you're going inside for the night!"

My mother handed us our burgers and people cooed and admired our matching bathing suits. We were always matching. Together we sat down on the pool deck to eat. Afterward, we got back in the water to play mermaids, again.

At some point my mother called us in to bed. We pretended to cry and begged her to let us stay up a little later. She didn't fall for it. We stomped up the stairs and went into the bathroom to strip out of our swim suits. I remember we decided to switch beds and dress in each others pajamas so we could play a trick on Mommy in the morning. It was our favorite prank and she deserved it for making us go to bed early when we weren't tired. Nevertheless, we fell asleep quickly.

The next morning, I woke up alone. I don't remember getting dressed or eating breakfast. What I do remember is spending what felt like forever walking around our house looking for Emily. The new renovations had yielded new hiding spots and it took me awhile to check them all.

I finally went to ask my mom, who asked my dad, who had just returned from dropping Eric at the airport.

"Paul, please tell me you took Emily with you to drop Eric off?!"

"No, why?" My dad's face paled instantly.

"Oh my God. Paul, we've looked everywhere, we can't find her."

My dad was already moving from room to room in the house checking all the places I had checked. By the time he returned, my dad was crying.

"Diane, call the police. Now."

That was the day my mother turned into something else. She never smiled or cried again.

But I did.

But I never cried as much as I did when Rocky died, which always made me feel bad and confused.

I remember a big police man talking to me, asking me what I remembered, had I heard anything in the middle of the night. He even asked if I liked having an identical twin sister or if I hated it. That question confused me for many years.

The days turned to a week and still no Emily. I slept alone in my room, switching from bed to bed, some nights pretending I was Emily and it was Rachel who was missing.

Lots of men with dogs came and went into the woods behind our house. Reporters were parked outside everyday and overnight. My parents wouldn't let me watch TV. The policemen tore up my bedroom and the rest of the house. I thought they were looking for a goodbye note. I thought Emily had run away. I was so mad at her.

Months went by and I grew lonely. I was excited when my birthday came. My mom cried from morning to night that day so my dad took me out for pizza. But he was quiet the entire time. My brother fell in love with a local and decided to stay in Japan. Since he was 18, my dad couldn't stop him. My mother missed him and Emily and drank wine and slept all the time. My father tried to be there to support me but he was suffering in his own way, I think. He upgraded Rocky's wooden cross to proper stone when I asked why

Emily hadn't had a funeral. I think he knew I needed a place to grieve. We all did.

One day he came home with a new dog which I named Naughty Boy. I hated Naughty Boy. He was trying to be Rocky and no dog could *ever* be Rocky. He eventually ran away. No one looked for him.

Four months after Emily disappeared, my father filled in the pool. I remember sitting in my room (which felt big and cavernous and cold) and watching them drain the pool. It took two days to fill it in with dirt. The pool had been the one last happy thing in my life. And my father had taken it away. He had taken my brother away too. He was the taker of things.

One afternoon, I was flipping through channels on the TV. The remote dropped from my hands when I suddenly saw my face on screen. It was a show called Unsolved Mysteries. My mother walked in then and saw what I was watching. I was afraid I was in trouble but she just gave me a blank look and walked right back out. I turned the TV off.

My parents began to yell at each other when they thought I couldn't hear. Their marriage was strained. There were so many phone calls from witnesses who reported seeing Emily somewhere. But they were almost always just seeing me. Whenever this turned out to be the case, which was often, my mother would give me an accusing look, like I had purposefully raised her hopes and then kicked the chair out from under her. Every false lead seemed to kill her a little more.

It was around then that I realized why no one liked me anymore. I was like a ghost, an echo of my sister. A pale shadow following around her mysterious disappearance. My parents could barely look at me. I know they think I didn't notice, but I did.

We eventually had a funeral for Emily, but I don't remember it very well. At least, not as well as Rocky's funeral. I just recall thinking how stupid it was to have a funeral for an empty box.

After a year, my mother filed for divorce. I still remember their very last fight. They were so far gone by then that they didn't seem to care that I heard.

"My brother would never hurt my children. Christ, what the hell is wrong with you, Diane? You can't just go around casually accusing people of serious crimes like kidnapping!"

"She's not kidnapped anymore, *Paul*, is she?" She spat at him. "She's dead! But I'm starting to think you already know that."

"How *dare* you say something like that to me? I love Emily. I loved all our children!"

"Yeah, I'm sure you loved Emily a lot. How much *did* you love her, Paul? Do I need to keep Rachel away from you, too?"

SLAP

I recoiled like it had been me he'd hit. I didn't understand what my mother had said. Tears poured down my face. Stupid Emily. Why couldn't she have just stayed in bed? Why did she have to go wandering off? Where did she go? Why had she done this to our family?

My thoughts were interrupted by a whisper from the next room.

"Why did you fill in the pool, Paul?"

I ran then. I didn't understand that question. I didn't want to understand.

Years went by. My mother met a new man named Bobby and moved out of our house. My dad and I maintained a strained but quiet home life - I avoided him at all costs. I spent more and more time at friend's houses and he spent more and more time in his study. The following summer, Dad built a deck over our filled-in pool. He never bought furniture for it.

When I was 13 I learned that my mom was living with Uncle Cliff, my dad's brother. I hated going to their house. Cliff had an above ground pool, and always tried to get me to go swimming with him. He even bought me swim suits, little bikinis that made me uncomfortable to look at. They would be laid out on the bed whenever I came to visit.

But I never went swimming with Uncle Cliff. I hated pools now. Soon they stopped inviting me to their house.

My dad was now spending every night shut up in his study, which he had moved to the room at the back of the house. He kept it locked and he would never let me inside.

I moved out when I was 18. My dad hugged me the day I left. It was the first time he had looked at me, much less touched me in seven years. He whispered that he loved me and then turned around and walked back into his study, closing the door behind him and locking it. I left.

Three weeks later a police officer showed up at my apartment. He sat me down and told me my father had been found dead.

I went to the house that night. My dad had killed himself in his study while sitting at his desk. I finally got to see the room - the body was gone, but the blood remained.

I looked around. The study was basically empty. There was a desk, a chair, seven photos, a notebook and a drawing. The desk sat in the middle of the room and faced the window to the backyard. The photos were of Emily and me. The drawing was one that Emily had drawn of our family shortly before she disappeared. The notebook was empty except for the last page. I read the title.

What happened the night of August 16th, 2002

But there was nothing written below it.

The chair was covered in blood but I was so numb I sat in it anyway. So it had been him. The whispers were true; it had been him all along. Our own father.

"What have you done?" I whispered.

I looked out the window and was surprised to find it situated over Rocky's grave. The tombstone was almost close enough the read.

"Ma'am? Ma'am, I know this is difficult. But I- I want to let you know that with this notebook we can get a warrant to excavate the yard."

I glanced up at the detective standing next to me. I knew he was trying to tread lightly. I nodded at him.

"But out of respect," he continued, "I want to ask you first."

I looked back out into the yard. I looked at the empty deck my father had spent an entire summer building and then never used. What was buried underneath it? I stood up and looked the detective dead in the eye.

"Dig it up."

I thought I knew what they'd find at this point. I thought maybe my mother had known it all along. But neither of us was right.

The excavation took 6 days. First, they had to tear up the deck. I stayed at the house that week, in my old room, and watched their progress from my bedroom window. The room didn't feel too big anymore. It felt small and suffocating.

I had my father quickly cremated and scattered his ashes in a ditch off the 405. I threw the urn in there too.

The first body was found at 11:29pm on a Thursday. I awoke to the sounds of yelling and dressed quickly. I ran down the stairs, through the door and out under the flood lights in the backyard. I darted my way around the mounds of dirt to where the forensics team was gathered. I braced myself and peered over their shoulders.

"That's not my sister."

They all turned to look at me.

"What is she doing here?" Someone said so no one in particular.

"That's not Emily." I tried again. Someone grabbed my arm then.

"Who is that? That's not my sister! Who is that?" I was yelling. I knew I was becoming hysterical, but I couldn't stop myself from screaming.

They dragged me away from the body. I sat next to the house wrapped in a blanket for the rest of the night. I didn't understand. Who was that? That wasn't Emily. Emily was me and that wasn't me. The bones were too big. They were too long. That wasn't Emily. Who was that?

At dawn, someone finally came to talk to me.

"Rachel-"

"Who is that?" I asked for the hundredth time that night.

"Rachel, we can't say for certain at this point but there's some strong evidence to suggest that the body might be, well that it could be...your brother."

"No," I said flatly, shaking my head. "Eric is in Japan. He's married. He's 30 now."

"Well, do you have an address? Or a phone number?"

"No... I mean...Eric doesn't talk to anybody anymore."

"Okay, well the M.E. took the body, so we'll know more soon. Just hang tight."

Just hang tight. What an absurd thing to say. The shitty world I had managed to build for myself from the ashes of my former life was starting to crumble.

Who was in the pool? The question haunted me for days. It wasn't Eric, it couldn't be. That much I knew. Unless Eric had come back from Japan. But I would know if he had, wouldn't I? Wouldn't he have come to see me?

I got my answers a few days later. Eric had not come back from Japan - because Eric had never left. Though his body had almost completely decomposed, the cheap, plastic "Good Luck" beaded necklace around his neck hadn't. The police ruled that he had died on the night of the party.

I didn't understand anything anymore. My mind refused to accept their findings. I began falling apart.

I wasn't there when they found the other body in the pool. It was Rocky's. When I walked into the house, they gave me his bones in an evidence box. It was all they had.

I looked down at the box and the dirty bones inside, and I knew where Emily was. I knew why my father had moved his office. I knew why he had replaced Rocky's cheap wooden headstone with a heavy one made of shiny white marble. I knew why he had inscribed it: *A Voice I Loved is Still.* I knew why the date didn't match Rocky's death.

Emily's small body was well preserved. When I saw how little she was I started shaking. I never remembered being so small. He had taken great care in burying her. She was inside a white bag I had never seen before, a special type I had never heard of. It had effectively mummified her. She was laying on her back in a dress with her small hands crossed and her eyes closed. She looked peaceful and beautiful.

I watched them place her gently on a metal board. I watched them zip a different bag over her. I watched them load her into a van. And I watched them take her away. I sat down next to the headstone. It was her resting place for the last 12 years. I looked through the window and I saw my dad's desk and his chair. I sat there all night. People brought me water and tea. But I just stared at the empty hole in the ground. Confused, angry and lost.

The excavation team left the next morning. The lead detective on Emily's case - a man named Beller - called me around dawn. Because of the state of Emily's body, they were able to collect evidence from her. They were waiting for it to cycle through the lab. I asked what kind of evidence. He wouldn't say.

The day I got the official report is another that I will never forget.

I was on the phone with my mother who I had finally found after months searching. She was in Philadelphia with Uncle Cliff and they had taken up heroin together.

I told her the police wanted to talk to her. I told her about Emily and Dad. I didn't tell her about Eric yet. I couldn't tell her that over the phone.

But she wasn't all there. She asked the same questions again and again. She repeated what I said. It was hopeless. I took down her number and hung up the phone. Detective Beller could deal with her.

As soon as I hung up, he called me.

"Rachel, we have the results of the autopsies, can you come down to the station?"

I sighed. It was late. After the conversation with my mother I was exhausted and emotionally drained. There was no way I would make it downtown tonight.

"Can you just tell me over the phone? I'm sorry, I can't, there's no way I can get there tonight."

"Where are you? I'll send a car."

"Actually, can you please just tell me? I can't...I can't go back there. I can't see their bodies again. I can't be in that room."

The detective paused then seemed to come to a decision.

"Rachel, there was semen on Emily's body."

"What?" I didn't hear that right...

"Yeah... We also found ligature marks on her neck. The Medical Examiner has ruled Emily's death a homicide."

"Yeah, okay, but-"

"There is no mistake."

"Yeah, but, can you say the first part again? Because I swear you said-"

"Rachel, your sister was raped."

No, no, no, no, no.

"My dad couldn't have-"

"The semen isn't a match to your dad. It's a match to your brother."

I didn't speak. I didn't move - until I started to shake.

"I wouldn't usually be so frank, but you've been through a lot and you deserve to know this. Here is what we have pieced together: on the night of August 16th, 2002 Eric went into your room and took Emily. He then drugged her, raped her and, accidentally we think, killed her by strangulation. Your father walked in on him and beat your brother to death. This all occurred in the late evening or early morning of the party. He then held the bodies for a month or so until he had the pool filled."

"My-my brother went to Japan-"

"No, he didn't."

"But my dad, he killed them-"

"No, he killed one of them. This is a crime of passion and, honestly, I'm not even sure your dad would have done time for it. I don't understand why he didn't just come forward."

I was silent. I knew why. It was because of me and my mom. Emily's disappearance had broken us but we'd always had hope. Hope that Emily would be released someday. Hope that she had found a new family. Hope that she would eventually come home. But she had never left.

And Eric, how could we reconcile our beloved Eric with the monster he truly was? My father had borne this knowledge and the burdens of it alone. His sacrifice may have been wasted on my mother but not on me. That hope for Emily, and love for Eric and my parents had gotten me through so much when there was so little ground to stand on. The cost he must have paid to do this for me - it was unfathomable.

And I had burned his body and scattered his ashes on a highway. He would never be laid to rest with the family he had endured so much to protect. And I had done this to him.

My father wasn't the monster. I was.

I filled a casket with the photos on my father's desk and the drawing he had held to his chest when he shot himself. And then I, too, buried an empty casket. I buried Emily next to my dad, and my mother on her other side two years later. I don't know what the state did with Eric's body and I haven't asked.

So really, this is a letter to you, Emily. To let you know why this happened and to tell you I'm sorry.

I'm sorry that when the monster came that night he choose you instead of me.

I'm sorry that I thought you ran away, and I'm sorry I never looked for you.

I'm sorry I abandoned the person who loved you the most to his demons. I'm sorry I left him forgotten and alone in a ditch.

I'm sorry I blamed you for destroying our family.

But most of all, I'm sorry that I'm the only one left standing.

THE AFTERLIFE EXPERIMENT

I've always felt a little lost in life, like I never received complete instructions on who I'm supposed to be. Everyone else around me seemed to know exactly who they were. Their lives would fly right by me; their GPS's locked on to destinations while I just sat idling in the street. In high school I never did any extracurricular activities because I couldn't figure out if I was a sports person or a music person. And it was no different in college. I wandered through four different majors, unable to decide who I wanted to be. I just felt like a blank slate.

And if I was a blank slate, Micah York was The Starry Night - authentic, beautiful, perfect. He was my exact antithesis which is what attracted me to him in the first place. He was born knowing *exactly* who he was and what he was about. His confidence and certainty in himself was an all but tangible element of him.

We first met in our freshman year of college; he was a Neuroscience student and I was majoring in History. We dated our sophomore year, after I changed my major to Computer Sciences. We broke up in our junior year, just before I decided I wanted a degree in Psychology, instead. And he asked me a favor our senior year, just after my guidance counselor told me it was too late to switch majors again.

Our last semester of college was beginning soon and Micah had been applying to grad schools. He wanted to get his Masters in Neurobiology and I helped him with the applications when I had time. I knew Micah was under a lot of stress to nail his senior thesis so I was surprised when he asked me over to his house for a "party" that January. I should have known something was up because Micah was a meticulous student and he didn't throw parties – ever.

When I arrived at his off campus apartment, I considered not even getting out of the car. His flat was dark and quiet, there was definitely no party. Just what was he up to? I picked up my phone to call Micah and beg off but curiosity suddenly got the better of me and I hung up.

When I walked into the familiar TV-less living room I saw two familiar faces and two strange ones.

There was Micah, of course, and Micah's friend Sean Nichols, an Organic Chemistry major. The other two people were introduced to me as Irina Bradley, another med student, and Holly Bishop, a Philosophy major.

Irina the med student scooted over and made room for me on the couch. I sat down hesitantly and waited for Micah to begin whatever it was he was doing. He rose and walked to the middle of the room.

"Thanks for coming, guys. I'm sure you're wondering why you're here because, clearly, this isn't a party. The truth is I have something of vital importance to ask each of you."

Micah paused, for effect I'm sure, took a deep breath and dropped his voice an octave.

"I have selected each of you to take part in the greatest experiment of not only your lives but perhaps even in human history. I am asking you to take part in my doctoral thesis."

I rolled my eyes. Classic Micah. He may be many things, but humble wasn't one of them. Jackass appeared to be, though.

"And what is your thesis?" I asked him nonchalantly, as if his previous statement hadn't been utterly stupid.

"A conclusive essay detailing what happens after human death."

Irina the med student laughed. Sadly, I knew Micah well enough to know he was being serious.

"How do you intend to prove anything?" I asked. "What kind of experiments have you designed?"

"Well, Bridget, I'm going to kill myself."

The room fell quiet and Micah, mistaking the shocked horror for awed silence, stood a little taller and finally smiled.

"You can't be serious."

"Oh, I am and it's completely reversible. I am going to be the first person in the *world* to prove or disprove the existence of an afterlife."

"We," demanded Sean.

"Yes, we. This paper is going to be our ticket into any university in the world. Wars have been waged for centuries over deities and religions and we are going to prove what is scientifically correct beyond a shadow of a doubt!"

"You're an idiot," I sighed and rose from the couch to leave. Irina followed me but Micah beat us to the door.

"Bridget, wait! At least hear all of it before you walk away. Please."

I narrowed my eyes at him and shook my head.

"I want no part in killing anyone. Even you."

"I'd like to hear how it works." Holly the Philosophy major coolly cut in from her spot on the couch.

"Ah, actually, it's something *I* developed." Sean said. "A cocktail of biological and non-biological chemicals. It's been tested and it's safe."

"*Tested?*" Irina asked in horror. "On whom?"

"On local wildlife."

"So never on a person." I said.

"Not yet but it *is* safe." Sean said quickly.

"So then how *does* it work?" Irina asked. She took a step back toward the couch and that's when I knew they had her.

Micah gestured to Sean.

51

"I've developed a poison and a biologic. I call them the Romeo and Juliet serums. Juliet is a poison that kills the body. Romeo is a biologic, or antidote for lack of a better word, that revives it."

"Clinical death will only take place for 30 seconds." Micah cut in. "No brain damage, no organ damage."

"Yes, it truly is perfectly safe; the body will only be dead for a short time." Sean confirmed.

"So, Flatliners." I glared at Micah.

"What?" Sean asked.

"Flatliners, it's a movie. The characters kill themselves and bring themselves back. If I recall it didn't work out too well for them in the film. But Micah knows that since he's obsessed with it."

"That's a Hollywood movie." Micah said, dryly. "This is legitimate science."

"No, you're Kiefer Sutherland," I pointed at him, "he's Kevin Bacon," I pointed at Sean, "and I'm Julia fucking Roberts!"

"No," Micah said hotly, "actually *she's* Julia fucking Roberts!" He pointed to Holly.

"So am I Oliver Platt, then?" asked Irina.

"No one is Oliver Platt!" Micah yelled.

"Well, if we get to choose I'd rather be Oliver Platt than Kevin Bacon." Sean interrupted.

"Sean, you're fucking Kevin Bacon." Micah spat.

"And you're Keifer Sutherland!" I yelled at him.

"THIS ISN'T FUCKING FLATLINERS!"

I sighed. "So I'm not going under."

"No." Micah looked exasperated.

"Then why am I here?"

Micah combed his hand through his dark brown hair. "Jesus, I've been trying to get to that."

"Am I going under?" Irina asked.

"No, just me, Sean and Holly."

"And you think *she's* going to agree with that?"

"Actually," Holly interrupted, rising from the couch. "I already have."

"Why?" I gaped at her.

"Because I want to know, I *need* to know why I'm here, why any of us are here. I want to know what the soul is and where it goes, I want to hold the keys to human existence, love and suffering, life and death. I want to understand our purpose. And I'm getting paid and it's perfect for my dissertation."

"That's another thing," Micah said quickly, "everyone will get paid."

"How much?" Irina narrowed her eyes at him.

"$500 each."

I groaned. $500 was pretty much how short I was on tuition for this semester and Micah knew that. What an ass.

"The Romeo and Juliet serums are safe. They've been tried and tested and they *will* work. Sean and I have rented a house on Emerald Street to conduct the experiment. All I need, all I'm asking, is for you to show up, Bridget. Just show up next Saturday."

"And what about me?" asked Irina.

"Irina, I need you to administer the serums and monitor vital signs. Look guys, this whole thing will take less than a minute and then you guys can walk away with your five hundred dollars and a credit on my thesis."

"And what makes your evidence, which is pretty much just your testimony, conclusive?" I asked.

"The serums Sean developed will be available to anyone and everyone and they can repeat my experiment at their leisure."

"But I don't think that-"

"Please, Bridget, just show up on Saturday."

There wasn't one facet of this little science experiment that didn't make me profoundly uncomfortable. But the way Micah looked at me, the tension in the room, the five hundred dollars...

"I'm not asked, Bridget. I'm begging." Micah grabbed my hands and squeezed.

"I'll think about it."

***

I wasn't really surprised to find myself at the house on Emerald Street that following Saturday. I'd debated about it all week but in the end - all other factors not withstanding - I was curious. Micah was brilliant, top 1% of his class, several published papers; what if he was right? What if he did see something? People have near death experiences everyday and came back with stories. Micah was going deeper into death than anyone ever had ever come back from before and he was doing it in a controlled environment using an experiment that could be easily duplicated. I mean, who knows?

Micah greeted me at the door with a smile that said he knew I'd come and walked me to the large, barren living room. It sported tan walls, hardwood floors, lots of hospital equipment and 3 cheap looking twin beds.

Sean and Holly were already laying on two of the beds with nervous smiles on their faces and IVs in their arms. Irina was bustling around checking equipment and looking incredibly stressed.

Micah handed me an expensive looking, heavy camera. "The cameras at the end of our beds are already recording – they're our static cameras. I need you to walk around and record with this one as well. Irina is going to stagger our injections so that she can handle all three of us. You are simply a witness, nothing more."

"Okay... Micah, are sure you want to do this?"

"Bridget, we've been testing this and as long as Romeo is injected in under a minute, which it will be, there is no risk."

"There's definitely risk, Micah. And near death experiences-"

"This isn't a *near* death experience, it's a *death* experiment. Look, I know you're worried, and that's why I wanted you here, to make sure nothing goes wrong. And even if it does, I have stacks and stacks of notes and narratives proving that this was *my* experiment."

"Yeah, but..."

I couldn't think of anything else to say. Any objection I had, Micah would have an answer for. That's just the way he was. There was no stopping him now; I could either be here to see it or be somewhere else to hear about it. I chose to stay.

Micah walked over to stand in front of the static camera.

"It's 12:51pm on Saturday, January 14th. I am Micah York and this is the first attempt of the afterlife experiment."

Micah walked over to his bed and sat down, letting Irina expertly thread a needle into his vein. He lay back on the pillow and turned to Sean and Holly.

"Remember, guys, as soon as you regain consciousness speak directly to your cameras about what you saw."

"Yep."

"Got it."

"Okay guys," Irina said with a shaky voice. "Everything is ready."

"Alright," Micah said, excitedly, "30 seconds, that's all. Irina, as soon as the last of the Juliet leaves the tube, hit this timer."

Micah pointed to the digital clocks that were set to 00:30 at the head of each bed. Irina nodded.

"Bridget, you film." I swallowed loudly and nodded too.

"See you on the other side," Micah smiled and gave a thumbs up to Holly and Sean who returned it and then settled back on their beds. I hit record.

Irina picked up three red tubes of thick, clear liquid from a nearby table. Steadying her hands, she slowly injected the first tube into Micah's IV, and then hit the timer above him. At the exact moment she did, Micah's heart-rate monitor flat-lined. I jumped at the high-pitched squeal and tried to steady the camera.

Irina hurriedly moved over to Sean and did the same for him and then Holly. Now all three EKG machines were loudly flat-lining. Irina put her hands over her ears for a minute and then pointed to a different monitor.

"Get this! Bridget, record this!" It was Micah's EEG and there were zero active brain waves. "Get Holly and Sean's too!"

I could suddenly taste a bitter metal in my mouth and I knew I was beginning to panic. This had been a bad idea, a very bad idea. By the time I looked back over to Micah's timer there was 8 seconds left on it. Irina had already loaded up a green tube, the Romeo biologic, to Micah's IV and was just waiting to push it in.

The chorus of all three EKG machines wildly sounding their alarms was deafening. It was screaming at us: "Do something! DO something! Why are you just standing there? Save them!"

Just when I couldn't stand it anymore, a different alarm buzzed and Irina injected the Romeo into Micah's arm. I didn't breathe at all as I waited for Micah's vital monitors to show life. It took less than 5 seconds for the EKG machine to register a spike. And then another. Micah's EEG machine suddenly flared to life as well. I exhaled.

Irina had just stepped over to Sean when Micah suddenly shot up in bed, eyes wide, and opened his mouth. I was so excited and curious that I almost forgot to hold the camera up. I couldn't wait to hear what he had to say.

But Micah didn't say anything. He just screamed. The surprise and force of it made me stumble back into a wall. It was the most blood-curling scream I had ever heard. And then, Sean started screaming, too. Micah took no notice of him and threw himself off the bed to the floor, slamming his head on the wood over and over again. Sean had also jumped out of bed and run over to the wall to stand just 2 inches from it, screaming at it, as if he didn't know the wall was there.

My shock quickly gave way to panic. Micah's head was already bloody and the sound it made against the hard oak was sickening.

"Irina, help me!"

Irina, who hadn't moved since Sean had knocked her out of the way, stared at me wide-eyed.

"We need to get him off the floor, he's hurting himself!"

She opened her palm and looked down at the last tube of Romeo biologic as if she'd never seen it before.

"You didn't give that to her yet?! Give that to Holly! Now!" My voice was high and wild. I was holding Micah in my arms while he continued to hit his head against the air, as if the floor were still there. And the screaming, oh God, the screaming.

Both Micah and Sean were splitting my ears open. The horror on Micah's face as he beat his head harmlessly against the air, mouth open in a wide O and the sharp, agonizing terror coming out of Sean was enough to make me my eyes well up in fear. What had happened? What had they seen?

The camera, long forgotten, lay discarded under Micah's bed where his flailing legs had kicked it. Irina was doing frantic chest compressions on Holly, tears streaming from her eyes. But I knew it was too late, Holly was lost.

"Irina, Irina, call 911." She didn't stop working on Holly, just continued on like she hadn't heard me. And perhaps she hadn't. The screaming...

I let go of Micah just for a moment to grab my phone and he was up and running. He hit the front door and smashing his forehead against the glass.

"Micah, stop!"

If Sean noticed us near him, he didn't show it. He just continued that piercing, horrible scream.

Emergency services couldn't hear me on the phone but they had someone at the house within 5 minutes. A very, very long 5 minutes. Irina gave up on Holly at some point and just paced around the room mumbling "I don't understand. I did it right. I don't understand."

They took Sean, Holly and Micah away in an ambulance and they took me and Irina to the police station. They watched the videos.

I never graduated but at least I didn't go to prison like Irina. I retreated into myself after her trial and refused to speak to anybody. I spent months holed up in my apartment asking the same question over and over.

What did they see?

And it's not like I could ask them. Sean had screamed until he permanently lost the use of his voice. Now he sits in a room in a hospital facing a wall with his mouth wide open as if he were screaming. And somehow, that's worse than the screaming. He hasn't said or written a word since that day.

Micah, he's in a hospital too. Sometimes he screams and sometimes he's quiet. Sometimes he thrashes and sometimes he lies as still as the dead.

I have visited them both many times, begging them to tell me what they saw. But my visits were fruitless until this last time.

Yesterday when I visited Micah he was in his screaming stage.

I sat with him and let him scream waiting to see if he would transition to one of his catatonic stages so that I could speak. When I was tired of waiting I leaned in close to his ear and I asked him.

"Micah, what did you see?"

His screaming slowly morphed into an insane, uncontrollable laughter I'd never heard before. His doctor, who'd been just outside, came running into the room.

"What did you do?" He asked, alarmed.

"I just asked him a question." I responded, quietly.

"What was the question?"

"I asked him what he saw."

We both noticed the sudden silence at the same time. We slowly turned toward Micah to find him facing us, no expression on his face.

"It's all waiting for you. It's waiting for all of us." Then his mouth fell open into a large O and the laughter slowly began again followed by shrill, horrible screams.

I left the hospital that day wishing I had never come at all, wishing I'm never met Micah. I drove home with tears pouring down my cheeks. *What did they see? What's on the other side? Do I even want to know?* But it really doesn't matter anymore. Someday I'll find out. And so will you.

THE GLEN

I climb out of my car and survey the intimate piece of wooded glen before me. It's quiet here, and cold. I have come to this secret, isolated place everyday for the past week. It used to be Our Spot, but now, it is only Aiden's.

I sit on the grass and I stare at his tree and I feel the chilled, thin air whip the hot tears from my cheeks. I shake my head to try and clear it as the familiar questions bleed into my mouth, begging to be asked. How could he have done this? What drove him to it? Why didn't I see the signs? Is it my fault? I bury my head in my hands, partly for warmth, partly in despair. We were happy once, we were in love. This was Our Spot. And now when I look at Aiden's tree, all I see is death. And so I'll sit and contemplate our short time together and try to reconcile it all as I have done everyday since it happened.

3 months ago

I don't remember a time that I didn't love him. We went to preschool together and I watched him from afar. Our parents weren't friends or neighbors, we just happened to live in the same school district. I spent a decade loving him in silence. In high school, he joined a band and was well-liked. He was cool without even trying, one of those types. I was the shadow in the hallway, the unregistered blip on the lunchroom radar. I was something to step around, just a dismissive object out of the corner of their eyes. But, I had my own friends and they were as diffident as I was.

The first words I ever said to him were: "Thanks, you don't have to do that if you don't want to, even though you offered to."

Stupid words. Asinine words. The words of a child. I had dragged my friends to a party and Aiden was there. We had never drunk alcohol before but wanted to be accepted as one of their own, so we sipped on their wine coolers. Except Annie. Annie didn't sip, Annie got drunk. We tried to hold her up as best we could and Aiden saw our struggle. He wasn't drinking. He was so responsible, so mature. He offered to drive us home. I didn't have my car. We said yes.

I watch the wind dance between the branches of Aiden's tree. The long, spindly boughs are barren and with nothing to catch the gales, they move only slightly, as if slow dancing with a lover. It doesn't remind me of us. Your tree is strong, but then, it had to be, didn't it? I wonder how long it takes a man to die, hanging from a tree. I pull my jacket around me tighter as if it was a safety blanket, but it can't protect me from the questions. Where were the red flags? What does it say about me that I missed them? That I missed all of them?

2 months ago

Aiden called me and invited me to a horror movie. How did he even get my number? I suppose the way cool people get things that they have a mild interest in - passively and with minimal effort. We sat in the back of the theater. I tried to get my courage up to touch him, but I was failing. And then, at the first jump scare, I grabbed his arm, involuntarily. His hand immediately closed over mine and he held me there, smiling and stroking my fingers. Afterward we sat in his car and talked for hours. He was nothing like I'd thought. He was humble and creative and deep. And he showed me a smile I'd never seen on him before. I called it My Smile, because it was only ever for me.

I wanted to hide that we were dating from the school but Aiden didn't care, he wanted the world to know. After two weeks I met his parents and he met mine. He drove me to Our Spot after a party and kissed me for the first time. His lips tasted like cool mint. Our Spot...it had been my favorite place to go, in real life and in my dreams. It had been beautiful and warm, the magic of our young love reflected in a twinkling canopy of stars and shimmering, red autumn leaves.

But now it was just a grotesque pile of dirt and dead grass upon the skin of Mother Earth. The trees, once whimsical and droll, now looked like sharp, unwelcome daggers jutting intrusively out of the tender, hallowed ground. It looked like it hurt. If I could, I would tear the trees from her body and fill in the holes with soothing, white snow. Oh Aiden, I need to know why you did it! Why did it have to end? What drove you to such extremes?

Did he do it because of me? Or had it been buried deep within him all along?

I stare at Aiden's tree, willing it to give me the answers I crave, but the tree is silent and lovely, masquerading as an innocent, peaceful life. But I know it's not. It has played its part.

I loved you, Aiden. I told you so under this tree, and you told me, too. We were stronger than the demons, together, I know we were. How could someone like you, so loving, so creative, so beautiful wind up here - hanging from an ugly Sugar Maple, your body as empty as it's crisp, black branches? I had been so blind. To him and to what was slowly happening around me.

1 month ago

I can't put a finger on exactly when it started or why. It's like trying to remember the precise moment you fell asleep upon waking the next day. The details are hazy and blurred, it seemed to happen over time and yet all at once. He still winks at me, he hugs me. We go places together and we kiss. But the smile he reserved only for me seems to have disappeared from his stock of facial expressions. I don't realize then that I'll never get to My Smile again.

After a week, I begin to wonder if he is falling out of love with me. So I offer him the only thing a girl like me has to offer someone like that. My innocence. Aiden smiles gently and asks if that's what I really want. I tell him yes. I know that the night will be painful and beautiful and that I will blossom into something different and lovelier by the morning. He considers for awhile and then strokes my hair and tells me he wants nothing more. He promises not to hurt me. He promises not to touch me if I don't feel right about it when the time comes. He keeps his promise. We choose a night after a party to drive to Our Spot. I am happy again, for a short time.

The light in the sky is growing dimmer, now. Colors begin to bleed into the horizon and I know I must go soon. The wind has left Our Spot and the air, though thin and cold, is somehow stagnant. Had Aiden's last breath of air been like this: stale and decaying? Or had it smelled beautiful as Our Spot once had, like fresh pine and starlight? I would find no honest answers here. Only lies or silence.

7 days ago

I find it cruel, whether intentional or careless, that Aiden bought the rope while I was with him. I met him at the Home Depot where he worked and he said he had to buy something after he got off the clock. He said it like it meant nothing at all. It was a long, white rope, just an innocuous weaving of fibers, selected unceremoniously from a red bucket of ropes. How could such a plain, ordinary thing take away something so precious to me? How could it dare? It was nothing, just a bland, boring and common coil of rope- limp and lifeless. It had millions of brothers and sisters in the world just like it. It just doesn't seem fair, like it assumed too much of itself, to take something so important away. I wonder where the rope is now.

We went to the party, my last party with the man I loved. Unlike Aiden's sudden, yet somehow gradual change I can pinpoint the exact moment I knew something was wrong that night. Aiden stood across the room from me, whispering with strangers and staring. It was an odd gaze. He didn't try to hide his stare yet somehow still seemed ashamed of it. I began to feel sick then. It was my first and only red flag. I finally had a sign that something terrible was going to happen. But it was too late then.

I remember more than I wish to. Aiden noticed my state and helped me stumble to a bedroom. Four men followed him in. Aiden was true to his word, and never touched me. Perhaps there is comfort in that. A different man tied me with the familiar, course rope. It hurt my wrists. Funny thing that it is that pain I concentrated on more than any other.

The man I loved stood in the corner and watched it all. He smiled and laughed with them as the men did the disgusting things they did. Through the mist I could see them and I tried to remember every detail but halfway through it all my brain shut off as if there were a sudden power outage in my body. And the things they did in the dark...

When I awoke I was laying on the floor in a darkened room. The rope, like the very core of myself, had turned from snow white to a hot, unfamiliar red.

I didn't get to take Aiden to the Home Depot but that's okay, I bought the things I needed with his store discount anyway. Then, I convinced him to get in my car. Then I convinced him to drink a Mountain Dew. Then I drove him to Our Spot and penetrated him four times with four ordinary, common nails I had chosen at random from an ordinary, common black bucket. I found out that day that I enjoy poetic justice. Once he was stuck to the tree I sat down in front of it and watching him writhe for awhile. I thought he would be dead by the next day. But he wasn't.

I get up now and walk across the glen. Our Spot has changed as I have changed. Where I had once been clean and white and pure, I was now dirty and red and noisy. The glen had once been lively and busy with red-orange leaves dripping with so many promises. But now it was white and quiet and dead. The glen and I had stolen from each other, swapped our souls in the dead of night.

I step up to Aiden's tree. His wounds are no longer bleeding which disappoints me because I am still bleeding. Pieces of his feet are missing and chucks of flesh from his face and thighs, just as chunks of myself are gone. We are inside-out mirrors of each other and this calms me.

Aiden hasn't moved since I've been here. It seems that the elements and dehydration have finally killed him. I give a satisfied smile. I call it Aiden's Smile. I pull off an orange glove and place my hand against the thin, waxy skin of his face. He opens his eyes just a fraction and parts his cracked lips to speak. He makes no sound as there is only ash in his throat where his promises were cremated. I frown and sigh in disappointment as I prepare to make the drive home. I had hoped this would be the last I'd see of Aiden's Spot. I guess I'll come back tomorrow.

GIN AND TOXIC:
AN IN-DEPTH LOOK AT THE WEST CANYON CITY DOG TRACK MURDERS

If you are ever in Arizona and find yourself on the Interstate-17, pay attention when traveling through a town called West Canyon City. With a population just over 2,000, and nothing to recommend it to highway travelers but a small gas station, most people will drive right through this little community without a second glance. But if you slow down and look to the east of the highway, you may see a dilapidated, crumbling building with the simple words "DOG TRACK" written on the side in faded, orange lettering.

You have found the West Canyon City Dog Track, the site of one of the worst massacres in Arizona history. The property has remained derelict and neglected since the 80's, slowly rotting away on the hilltop where it was once a thriving den of debauchery.

If you were to exit the highway and park on the corner of Red Rattle Rd and Blaucher Canyon you could walk to the abandoned building and explore the stale, decaying ruins of a once popular greyhound track.

If you approach the side of the building with the fading orange letters you will see a silver gate standing open. If you venture through you will come to an unlocked door into the building. If, by chance, you are on the north side of the building, you will instead find a smaller doorway, this one with the door torn off the hinges. Graffiti to the left of this door reads "Why didn't you kill yourself today?"

If you then venture inside, you will find yourself in a cavernous, crumbling lobby. You will find a booth for reservations, a wall of betting windows and even a bar. Beyond that, you can explore the kennels, the private offices of the management, and even the overgrown dog track below.

Of course, one of the first things you'll see are the grandstands; rows and rows of red and yellow plastic seats, many of them still attached, while others have been torn up and thrown in an unceremonious pile nearby. This part of the building has an unsettling feeling as thousands of seats, all eerily expectant, face an empty field of weeds and a small mountain range beyond through large, broken panoramic windows. A large, metal sign hanging above tells you that the red seats cost 50 cents while the yellow seats cost 75.

If you continue to wander, you will find more graffiti such as "I know why she did it" and "Robert's secrets kill us all". You will no doubt finish your tour feeling unsettled and ill, and with good reason.

The story of this dog track is mysterious and difficult to find, having been intentionally and systematically erased from history.

Our story begins with a citrus farmer named Michael T. Lewis. In 1942, tired of his Tucson farm, Lewis opened a successful race track in Mexico called "Lewis Family Race Track", which was the first combination horse/dog track in North America.

It was enormously successful and with his new found wealth, Lewis moved his wife and four young children - William, Maggie, Maxwell and Robert - back to Arizona and opened several more thriving greyhound tracks.

The Lewis children grew and while William and Robert followed in the family business, Maggie and Maxwell showed little interest and went off on their own paths. Maggie married a young entrepreneur named Rex Taylor and Maxwell became a university professor.

Robert and William moved around the country opening tracks in Georgia, Washington and Montana. Michael, impressed by his son's excellent work ethic, named Robert President of the Arizona race tracks, of which there were four.

Robert, an aggressive but inexperienced businessman, decided in 1965 to open a new greyhound track in central Arizona. He chose a sleepy, rural town called West Canyon City, less than an hour north of Phoenix.

When his father wouldn't approve the funds to build this track, Robert found funding through a Rhode Island company called Imperial Racing Inc., a well known mob-run enterprise on the east coast.

With their help, West Canyon City Dog Track was opened in 1967, much to the chagrin of the locals, a devoutly religious group, who were horrified to find their pious town host to such a sinful sport.

Robert brought his sister and her husband to live in West Canyon City and oversee the track's management. Maggie's husband Rex was excited about greyhound racing and so Maggie found herself once again enslaved to the family business. She noted in her diary that year how much she hated dog racing and how much she resented her family for forcing this life on her.

The track was an enormous success despite local protests and harassment by the town's small police force. Gamblers from Phoenix would drive up on the weekends to get out of the heat and spend time drinking and betting at the greyhound track.

In 1973 Robert left Arizona to open a new property in Las Vegas, leaving Rex and Maggie behind to run the West Canyon track. Maggie strongly objected to being "abandoned in the middle of nowhere" but Rex was excited about the chance to run the business alone.

Robert didn't return to West Canyon City until early in 1982, when Maggie called him to complain about the increased tensions between locals and track management. In the years he had been gone, the protests had turned to vandalism, death threats and finally violence after a flaming bag weighted with a brick was thrown through his pregnant sister's window.

Rex and Maggie argued to shut the track down, citing violence and poor profit margins. Robert would not agree to it. He was by this time deeply in debt to Imperial Racing and they were no longer asking nicely for their money. The threats had grown so violent that Robert showed up in Arizona with his humerus broken in three places.

When her brother refused to release the Taylor's from their obligations, Maggie begged Robert permission to leave, telling him about a local man who was harassing her named Brad Davidson. She said she didn't know him and had no idea why, but that he followed her when she was alone and came to the track everyday to try and speak with her. He was an alcoholic and a gambler, she said. In April, a man accosted Robert in the street claiming to be Brad Davidson, and pleaded with him for help, claiming he was the real father of Maggie's baby.

In May of 1982, Rex and Robert got into a violent fist fight in the management offices when the latter went through the track's accounting. Robert accused Rex of running the track into the ground due to gross financial mismanagement. Robert was so angry that he told Rex about his conversation with Brad Davidson. Rex broke the cast off his brother-in-law's arm.

Robert was taken to the hospital to have his arm reset but the local ER staff refused to help him because he was the man who had "brought the very devil himself" to their town. Police were called and they escorted Robert off hospital property, roughing him up a bit. They told him that crime in their community had gone up ten fold since he had "invited all the sinners" down upon them.

The following month, Robert received another convincing threat from Imperial Racing to ruin him and decided on one last ditch effort to revive the track. Attendance had dwindled to almost nothing due to patrons being harassed and assaulted by locals as they came and left the dog track.

Robert bought ad space in Phoenix and Tucson and advertised the "comeback of the century" for the West Canyon City Dog Track. On July 10th of that year, all patrons of the track would not only receive $10 in betting credit but also drink for free between 11am and 1pm. Much to Maggie and Rex's disappointment, the response was overwhelming.

When the day arrived, Robert and Rex had to open the track early. Though the races weren't scheduled to begin until 10am, hundreds of people showed up at the track just after 8 in the morning. Phoenix locals had organized their own buses to transport them in mass.

At 9am Bill and the general manager shared an opening-day drink down on the track, which Robert declined.

The morning of July 10th, 1982 was a scorcher and the decision to allow people to drink for free quickly became an expensive one. Bill opened the bar early, at 10am and by 10:30 the line for the bar wrapped twice around the lobby.

Robert, Maggie and another barman opened two more makeshift bars - one next to the outside grandstands and one on the other side of the lobby - to deal with the demand.

Every seat in the inside grandstand was taken and people fought for the outside seats as well. Around 150 people stood mingling around the lobby, watching the races from above and sticking close to the bar. They won money; they lost it, they laughed and cried and drank. By noon, the party was in full swing and everyone was in a boisterous and rollicking good mood.

The first sign something was wrong was around 11:45am when the lines for the bathrooms grew as long as the lines for the bar.

At around 12:20pm people in the lobby started to get sick. Only a handful at first. But within an hour people were vomiting where they stood - this quickly spread to the grandstands.

The general manager of the track, who was stuck behind the reservations desk, informed concerned patrons that it was simply a bad batch of liquor and that it would pass. When several people in the lobby began to seizure, Robert closed the betting counter to stop people from asking for their money back.

By 1:30pm, the first person was dead.

He was followed in quick succession by others - death spread like wildfire. Some were found to have dropped dead in the bathrooms, others simply never raised themselves out of their seats and died where they sat and yet others keeled over in the lobby, screaming in pain.

Local emergency services, who had finally been called after the first death, were slow to respond and by 4:30pm 618 people were dead and a thousand more were hospitalized. Tents were set up in the dirt parking lot and medical staff were called in from every town within a 200 mile radius. Of those that were hospitalized, another 381 people died just outside the dog track. The 999 deaths were ruled as poisonings.

Robert, Maggie and Rex all survived.

Robert, the first to cast an accusation, wrote a letter to his father the following day which included a timeline of events on the day of the murders and a paragraph detailing why he couldn't help but be suspicious of his sister. Maggie had appeared unfazed as so many people died violent deaths next to her bar, and had also gone to considerable lengths to ensure that the man called Brad Davidson, someone she claimed to hate, was served several free drinks.

Maggie, in turn, openly accused her husband of the murders, after every bottle of liquor in the building tested positive for Arsenic. She stated that on that day she had twice raised a glass of bourbon to her lips, only to have Rex slap it away. Peculiar, she mused, that he had suddenly become so concerned for her pregnancy when he never had before. Rex disagreed that this ever occurred.

Robert, a seasoned drinker, was also suspected of the murders due to his refusal of an opening day drink with his manager, a tradition that Robert had always taken part in. In fact, no one had ever seen Robert turn down a drink in his life. It was noted as odd at the time and even more so after the deaths.

Rex, for his part, quietly accused Imperial Racing Inc., as he had started to receive threats from the east coast company the week before.

Michael T. Lewis wrote in correspondence to a business partner later that year that *he* believed the towns religious zealots had organized the poisonings since they were the only ones to gain from it.

The governor of Arizona at the time ordered a hasty investigation and a purging of all mentions of the tragedy from the local media, thereby ensuring it wouldn't get picked up nationally.

Most of the families of the victims (those gamblers who even had families) were purportedly bought off and the FBI closed the investigation on July 16th. The governor was in the throes of his own scandal at the time (accusations of handing out Indian casino licenses in return for campaign donations) and didn't want more bad press for his state.

In the end, no charges were filed. The track was closed that day and abandoned until the mid-80's when William Lewis tried to revive the property as a Farmer's Market. He abandoned this venture two years later, after it failed to draw vendors.

Robert and his brother-in-law Rex gave up race tracks and opened a successful string of portrait studios throughout the southwest. Robert died in 2001 and Rex in 2009. Maggie and

Maxwell are the only Lewis children still alive today. No one has ever admitted to the murders.

Perhaps one of the more confusing aspects of this case is the fact that West Canyon City's well water was also found to be contaminated with high levels of arsenic in 1985. Today, residents of the town and local businesses are served by a private water company due to the toxicity of their ground water.

Sadly, the culprit in this case may never be known due both to the local authority's refusal to investigate the massacre and the federal government's disinterest in it. And even if someone did decide to reopen the 30 year old cold case, most of the evidence has probably decayed and been destroyed by time.

Of course, as you know, West Canyon City Dog Track still stands today and you can even visit the bar where almost 1,000 people met their deaths. If you do decide to visit, take your time walking the grounds. You may even stumble on betting tickets with the date "July 10th, 1982" printed on them, as I did the last time I was there.

Even the bar still stands, though it is hidden beneath a pile of detritus. If you do manage to dig it out you may even find an unopened bottle of gin. But I won't tell you not to drink it. I've always thought 999 was an unsatisfactory number.

THE CREEK

My brother Teddy died on December 11th, 1999 during our annual family Christmas party. He was 12 and I was 9. I wish I could say it wasn't my fault, but at the end of the day, the whole thing had been my idea.

I'm from Woodbury, Minnesota as is my entire extended family. Every Christmas my parents would host a holiday party to eat, drink and gossip. It was always a boring event but I loved seeing all my cousins. The adults usually stuck us kids in the basement or the loft but that year my brother convinced them to let us go sledding at the park instead.

We bundled up in our purple Vikings parkas and loaded up the sleds with blankets and our pockets with hand-warmer packets. Then me, my brother, and our cousins Mike and Jeff set off for the sledding hill which was about a half mile down the road.

As soon as we were out of view of the house, Teddy stopped.

"You guys wanna do something fun?" He asked.

"Hell yeah!"

"Of course!"

"I want to go sledding." I muttered.

"Yeah, well, sledding is for babies," said Jeff.

"That's what I was thinking too!" His brother added.

Teddy smiled. "Good. Because I want to take you guys somewhere *way* more awesome."

"Where are we going?" I asked nervously. "Mom and dad will get mad if they look for us in the park and we're not there."

"They wont look, they're too drunk," Teddy laughed.

"But-"

"I think we should go to Rocking Horse Creek." He added coolly.

Rocking Horse Creek was actually more of a small river than creek but it had been called that for as long as I can remember. The creek had been named by neighborhood kids who'd found an almost life-sized rocking horse sitting abandoned and half submerged in the water. No one knew where it had come from just as no one knew the actual name of the river. Because no one had ever been stupid enough to tell their parents that they went there.

"But Rocking Horse Creek is almost an hour walk from here!" I whined. I was already cold and didn't feel like walking that far.

Mike snorted. "Pfft, don't be a baby. There're extra blankets if you're cold plus hand-warmer packets in your pockets."

"Yeah," Jeff added, "and if you want we can pull you along in the sled just like the baby you are!"

Mike and Jeff laughed. But Teddy didn't and he punched Jeff in the arm.

"Stop it, you guys! I'm not a baby! And why go to the creek anyway? It's probably ice."

"Because it will look hella cool!" Teddy said.

"Yeah, I want to go!" said Mike. "We could tie our jacket strings to some sticks and go ice fishing!"

"Yeah!"

"Well, I'm really good at ice fishing," I lied, "So I *have* to go so I can help you."

"*Sure* you are." Jeff rolled his eyes.

The walk didn't take an hour; it was more like 35 minutes, though it did feel longer due to the cold. When we approached we saw that the river was indeed frozen over. The ice looked several feet thick, though it was hard to tell. Jeff and Mike were really excited about it and kept testing their weight on the thinner ice of the riverbank.

I sat down on my sled and drew a couple blankets around me. *I'm smaller than them so I'm colder*, I justified to myself. Ted, Mike and Jeff stood on the riverbank and threw rocks onto the ice to see if they could break it. When they failed to produce even the smallest crack, Jeff announced it was time to play Ricochet Dare.

I hated Ricochet Dare. As soon as Jeff suggested it I felt a cold stone drop into the pit of my stomach. Ricochet Dare was something we'd been playing since we were little kids. The rules stated that if you were dared to do something and you didn't do it the game would end and you would be the new "Wuss" (and this ridicule would go on for weeks or even months). However, if you did do it then you got to dare someone in return. Generally, the dares start off mild but with every round the stakes get higher. The game would only end when someone inevitably wussed out. And, of course, that person was usually me.

But not this time, I thought as I shrugged off the blankets and stood up, pushing my hat up from my eyes. I had to redeem myself and make Teddy proud. I had to show them I wasn't a baby.

"Come on!" Jeff yelled at me. "You go first!"

"Okay. What's the dare?" I asked with false bravado.

"Hmm..."Jeff said. "Okay, you have to take 3 steps out onto the ice."

I eyed the frozen river warily. "Three steps?"

"Yep, and not *baby* steps, real steps."

"Stop it, I'm not a baby!"

"Then prove it."

I took my first step lightly and paid close attention to the give of the slippery mass beneath me. There was none that I could feel and the ice made no sound of protest underneath my feet. I took the two last steps quickly and then turned around and half-skated back to shore. My brother gave me a huge smile and a high five.

I dared Mike to take 4 and half steps. Mike dared Ted to do 6 steps. Ted dared Jeff to do 10 steps. And then Jeff dared me to walk all the way to the opposite shore.

The ice hadn't made a sound since we had started the game, instead remaining as silent as death. Still, there was something unsettling stringing through the cold air and the silence.

I stalled for as long as I could, trying to decide if I should complain. Jeff's dare was actually two dares and I didn't think that was fair. Technically I would have to do it twice: once to get to the opposite shore and once to get back. I was afraid of falling through to the cold water I knew was raging by under the ice.

"Come one, don't be a baby, just do it." Mike said.

"Little baby-waby afraid of the icy-wisy?" Jeff mocked.

"Stop it you guys, I'm not a baby! This dare isn't fair - it's two dares!"

My voice was drowned out by Jeff and Mike's mock baby cries. I looked at Teddy for help but he was laughing. *Laughing.* My older brother didn't even attempt to stick up for me, he was joining in with them!

I felt my lower lip wobble and tears fill my eyes. *Don't cry! Babies cry, you're not a baby!* I jerked my head back to river so they couldn't see my red face and traitorous tears. I felt a sob begin to bubble up through my throat and I knew I couldn't let them hear it.

I would die before I'd let them see me cry.

I took a deep breath and ran across the ice as fast as I could. And for a moment I actually hoped I did fall through. They would be in so much trouble and they would feel so sorry that they'd made fun of me and called me a baby. With every slap of my boot I listened for the telltale sound of cracking ice. But none came and before I knew it I was on the other side.

I raised my fists in the air triumphantly and waited to hear their cheers. When I turned to look back, they were still standing in a circle together, laughing. They hadn't even been watching me. They missed the entire dare.

And I wanted to cry all over again.

I swallowed the tears and was about to yell that I wanted to go home. But just then, I noticed something dangling from the tree above them. How had I forgotten? I was the only one who'd noticed it and I realized it was my ticket to revenge and redemption. But who to dare?

I stood silently watching them as they joked with each other and pointed at each of them in turn, silently mouthing to myself.

"Eeny, meeny miny, moe, catch a tiger by the toe, if he hollers let him go, eeny meeny miny moe."

My finger landed on Teddy. *Good*, I thought. *He's supposed to be my brother, he deserves it the most.*

I cleared my throat.

"I dare..." I yelled across the small river, interrupting them. They turned to look at me, almost surprised to see me standing on the other shore. So they *had* forgotten about me.

"I dare," I started with renewed anger, "TEDDY to rope swing across the creek and land on this side."

There was silence as, in tandem, all three looked up at the rope hanging from the tree above them. During the summer we would take turns swinging on it and cannon-balling into the water; and if you pushed off the tree hard enough, you could actually make it to the other side of the creek. I'd seen my brother do it many times.

Teddy's eyes got wide and he looked at me as if I'd sentenced him to death. Jeff and Mike immediately started prodding him, telling him not to be a wuss. I smiled smugly from the other side of the river. I hoped he'd fail the dare. It'd be just what he deserved.

It didn't take much name calling for Teddy to climb the tree and grab onto the rope. He tested it a few times and then hung on it with all of his weight. It held like it always had.

"When I get over there I'm going to dare you to do jumping jacks in the middle of the creek!" He yelled at me. That's when I realized my mistake. If Teddy dared me to do that I would most certainly wuss out and then they'd tease me until Easter. I sent a silent prayer up to God that Teddy didn't make it to this side of the river.

"On three!" Mike yelled to Teddy.

I watched Teddy count silently to himself and then push off from the tree as hard as he could. He swung in a long, deep arc just like he always did. I watched the scene with my fingers crossed, hoping the rope wouldn't go far enough and that he would have to land back on the other riverbank, his dare unfilled and the game ended.

But I could tell immediately that he was going to make it and somberly stepped backward to make room for him to land.

And then suddenly the loudest sound I've ever heard before or since rang through the air like a gunshot.

GROAN

SNAP

Teddy broke through as soon as he hit the ice and the rope and tree branch followed him down into the darkness below. I felt my feet moving under me as I slipped and slid my way out to where he'd gone in, sheer panic crushing my chest like a vice. All three of us were on our bellies groping into the angry, jagged hole within 10 seconds. We searched the watery void but all we could feel was the tree branch below us. And within a minute, we couldn't feel anything at all- our hands and arms had gone numb.

Jeff pulled Mike and I to our feet and started running for the sleds.

"Leave his sled here, we need to get out of here now!"

I felt cold and dead. I stumbled blindly toward the sound of my cousin's voice.

"We need to save Teddy. I want Teddy. He's in the ice. We have to get mom and dad." But I was blubbering so badly by the end that I doubt they understood a word of it. And despite my slurred protests, I followed them through the woods, confused and cold.

But after a while I couldn't feel the cold anymore. I couldn't feel any pain, in my heart or my body. In fact, I couldn't feel anything at all.

Mike didn't say a word for the entire walk back but Jeff went on and on about the "plan".

We would just say that Teddy decided to go home before us and that he had said he was going to take a shortcut through the woods - the other woods on the far side of the road.

I just nodded for awhile, even smiled at his plan. God, to this day I don't know why I smiled. We were almost home by the time I began to process what he was saying.

"No. I have to tell dad to save Teddy." I told him. I was surprised by how flat my voice sounded.

Mike just kept walking forward in a daze but Jeff whirled on me.

"It's too late to save him but you can save yourself! It's your fault this happened because it was your dare. They will take you to jail for murder and put you on death row; it's an open and shut case. You can't tell anyone anything. *Ever.*"

And I don't know why, but I believed him.

The hardest part of the day wasn't watching my brother die or the long, cold walk home. The hardest part by far was pretending like nothing was wrong when we got there.

What do you mean you haven't seen Teddy? He should have been back by now, he started home an hour before us.

I couldn't keep my poker face for very long, though, and I started crying. My dad thought it was because I was so cold that my skin had begun to turn white.

The adults immediately mounted a search of the woods between our house and the park, which of course, turned up nothing. By nightfall they had called the police.

Search and Rescue searched the wrong woods for the next 24 hours because they believed our story. The sledding hill had been crowded that day but a couple of people were sure they'd seen us there.

The day after that they intended to search the other side of the forest - the side Teddy was actually on - but a blizzard rolled in overnight and that search was called off. My parents were told that where ever Teddy was, he was most certainly dead.

Parents in the neighborhood stopped letting their children play in the woods, even in the summer. My own parents wouldn't let me leave the house for a year. I grew up angry and spiteful. I hated everyone, but no one more than myself. I applied to college just to get away from my parents, whose constant love and support felt vile and wrong to me. I wished they would have another kid so they could give their love to someone deserving and stop talking about Teddy all the time.

I got into U of M. My grades sucked and I drank a lot. My parents pressured me to excel since I was their last horse in the race. I never returned their calls or emails.

I lived with the guilt; just barely, but I lived with it. If nothing else, I could take a bit of pride in the fact that I was surviving.

Drunkenly one night, I finally told a couple of my close friend's about it. They agreed that it wasn't my fault, that shit happens, and that Teddy wouldn't want me to dwell on it. I made the dare, but he climbed the rope.

That night was a turning point for me. After being validated by people who actually knew the truth, I cut back on the drinking and I picked up my grades for the last two semesters.

And somehow, it was enough to graduate.

A year later I got an invitation to an engagement party at my parent's house. Cousin Jeff was getting married to a girl he'd met in the navy and I was "invited to celebrate their love" with them. As much as I always hated going back home, I wanted to support Jeff. Somehow, just knowing that he was living a full life despite our shared burden made me feel hopeful, like I could too.

The party was quieter and more reserved than the parties my parents threw when we were kids. They had become less fun since Teddy's death: more refined, more somber. Jeff was quieter than I remembered, too, but he was clearly happy with his new fiancé, who seemed like a very nice girl. And though a wide smile was spread across his face, his eyes betrayed a certain guardedness, especially when he looked at me.

I got up the courage to talk to him only once. We shared an awkward hug and I congratulated him on his engagement and asked him about his brother. Jeff told me that Mike was addicted to heroin and living in Arizona somewhere. I said that it seemed Mike had never really recovered. Jeff said he didn't know what I was talking about and walked away.

I spent the rest of the party hugging relatives, making small talk and pretending to drink (sobriety is suspect in my family). After awhile I went outside to take in a cigarette and a moment of peace. And in the secrecy of the autumn air, I started to cry.

This party should be boisterous and loud. My parents should be lively and laughing. Mike should be running around the party daring people to take mystery shots. I should be cheerfully telling stories from college and talking about my plans for graduate school. And Teddy should be here instead of lying dead at the bottom of a river bed.

I flicked my cigarette under my car and wiped the wetness from my cheeks. I knew what I had to do and where I had to go.

I had to see the river that had haunted me since I was nine. Had anyone been back to Rocking Horse Creek? Was Teddy's sled still there? Had they replaced the rope? Had the creek dried up? This was my worst fear. It had secrets I didn't want to live to see revealed.

I lit another cigarette as I walked and began to list all the reasons this was a bad idea. I spent the hike either begging myself to find the strength to turn around or begging for the courage to continue on.

I arrived at Teddy's grave before I was ready.

The creek was loud and the water was moving quickly - recent rain in the area to blame, no doubt. The rocking horse itself was in bad shape. Only its head was visible above the water now and it was so rotted you could barely tell what it was anymore. No one had replaced the rope.

I sat down next to the creek and took it all in. It was hard to believe this was the same place from which I still woke up screaming. It seemed to have healed since taking Teddy's life. If it could heal, maybe I could heal too. The tree was so full you wouldn't think it'd ever lost a single branch. The creek innocently bubbled by, full of life and vigor. Everything here was so different than I remembered.

Even the rocking horse.

Where the toy had once been cheerful, almost animated, it was now just a morbid, misshapen head. Its eyes were pointed directly at me and they bore a soulless stare right through me. It sent an involuntary shudder through my body and I turned away from the horse's head in revulsion, I immediately saw what the horse had been looking at: a sliver of red plastic jutting out of the ground behind me.

Teddy's sled.

My reaction was visceral and I had to lean over and vomit in the grass beside me. It was real. It had happened. Had I been pretending it wasn't real? Was that why I had really come here? To pretend that the past was gone and didn't matter anymore? How could I forget that what this place really was?

I stumbled to my feet and began walking down the riverbank away from the buried sled, pausing every few feet to dry heave. I just wanted to get away from it, that thing that was all that remained of my brother. Everything that used to be Teddy lay at the bottom of the river now. I pulled a cigarette from my pack with shaking hands. As I tried to light it I tripped over something and fell forward, my cigarette rolling down the riverbank and into the water.

It was a rope. And I knew right away that it was Teddy's rope.

I kicked it away from me, it was worse than the sled. If I had anything left to throw up, I know I would have. The end of the rope lay deteriorating on the riverbank with the length of it disappearing into the murky water of the river. And maybe I am morbid or sick or crazy, but I suddenly I decided that I wanted to know, I wanted to see.

I crawled over to it and picked it up. It felt just as it did all those summers ago when I used to swing from it into the water as Teddy clapped from the shoreline.

I began to pull the rope out of the river.

The water was fast moving and the rope was heavy. The creek didn't want to give up its secrets so easily and it rebelled against my efforts. Still I pulled harder. Just as I felt I was coming to the end of it, something long and thin breached the surface of the river. I saw it for only a moment before the rotted rope snapped and it sank back into the dark abyss.

I almost dove in after it. But as I stood on the riverbank, my brain screaming at me, I realized what I'd almost done. What if that was Teddy? Would I want to see?

Breaking from my trance, I hurled the rest of the rope into the water and fled into the woods. My lungs struggled to draw breath and the trees began to spin around me. I anxiously lit yet another cigarette and let the shudders wrack through my body as I waited for the nicotine to calm me.

I stood there, in the middle of the woods, the broken rope 20 feet behind me at the bottom of the river and took short drags off my cigarette. And when my breathing had become bearable again, I felt someone watching me.

It was Teddy, of course. He sat with his back against a tree, faded purple parka still bright in the mid afternoon sun, and in some parts bleached almost as white as his bones. Ripped foil from an opened hand-warmer packet was clutched in his hand, still remaining after all these years. He stared at me accusingly; the deep eye sockets of his skull were somehow not empty, instead they held a knowing consciousness that said he knew what we had done. He knew we'd left him to die.

But we hadn't known that, Teddy! We hadn't! We didn't know you crawled out of the river. We didn't know you were freezing to death as we ran home to bury our secrets! We would have saved you, Teddy, if we had known. You know that. We had blankets and sleds, if we had known you'd crawled from the river, we would have saved you!

I yell this at the skeleton, in my head or out loud I'm not entirely sure. But Teddy just sits there staring me; thirty yards from the rocking horse, twenty yards from the broken tree. And I know he'll sit here forever. Because Jeff and Mike don't need to know that our sins are more terrible than we'd ever thought. I know it is my burden to bear. And I can tell as he watches at me in the fading sunlight that Teddy agrees.

THE LOST TOWN OF DEEPWOOD
PART 1

When I was a kid my dad traveled a lot for work. Back then, his company was growing exponentially and my father was sent to oversee the opening of new stores all across the country. In 2002, he had a particularly busy year. My dad was assigned to a store in Pennsylvania and, because it was a longer assignment and because it was summertime as well, he decided to take my mom and me with him.

Since we were going to be there for two months, they gave us a fully furnished house in the suburbs. It was two stories tall and at the end of a very lonely cul-de-sac. The town itself was very small, with a little over 3,000 residents, and the suburb where we stayed was even more rural.

Our neighborhood was relatively new, and most of the houses were still empty. The housing development, Lone Wood, had only just started cutting into the dense forest that surrounded it and all the empty houses gave it a very eerie, albeit boring, feel.

Lucky for me, there were a few other kids who lived in Lone Wood and one of them happened to be my age. Jamie and I were both 12 and really that was all we needed to have in common.

We had a lot of fun that summer. Being a city kid, I was eager to explore all the bike trails local kids had made out in the woods. The city of Middlesbrough was a very old town which was incorporated sometime in the early 1800s. The town had tons of history, but nothing really to do. One particularly boring Sunday, Jamie and I even went to the town's museum.

It was pretty boring, as expected, until we heard some kid ask an employee about the "lost town". The employee replied that that was just a legend, but that was enough to pique my curiosity.

I quizzed Jamie about it but he didn't seem to know much either. It was a full five weeks into the summer before I finally got my questions answered.

Jamie and I were building a bike ramp over a narrow stream late one afternoon when we saw a group of five teenagers boisterously heading out into the woods. They were carrying flashlights and beer, several of them trying to scare the girls of the group into turning back.

"I wonder where they're going." I mused as I glanced over at Jamie. He stood up and wiped his brow.

"I know where they're going."

"Where?" I stood up and dusted the dirt off my shorts. The novelty of living in a small town had weeks ago given way to boredom and I jumped on anything that sounded remotely interesting.

"They're looking for the Lost Town." He sighed regretfully.

"Okay, seriously, what is that? I knew you know more than you let on. I need to know Jamie, I need to know!" I shook his shoulders in mock hysteria and he stumbled for balance.

" Alright! I'll tell you, geez, Katie!" Jamie picked up his bike and started walking down the bike path. I grabbed mine and followed him.

"The Lost Town is just a dumb legend. The stories say that Middlesbrough had a sister city nearby, somewhere out in these woods. Then one day, like a century and a half ago, the whole town just disappeared. The people left or died, nobody knows, nobody even remembers the name of the town. It's like a right of passage or something for kids to go looking for it."

"Jamie we should-"

"No!" He stopped and turned to look at me. "Some kid went looking for it in the 70s and never came back. They found his body like ten years later in the middle of nowhere. He got lost out there. It's easy to do, everything looks the same."

"He was a total idiot! Probably on drugs, it was 70s. We are a totally different generation - we have satnav!"

"Satnav?" He looked at me curiously. Jamie had lived in this town his whole life and sometimes I forgot how sheltered he was.

"Satellite Navigation? My dad has a GPS that he totally wouldn't notice missing for a day. Come on Jamie, it'd be so much fun!"

"I'd better get back." Jamie looked at his watch and then mounted his bike. "My dad is taking me to a movie tonight."

We rode in an uncomfortable silence until an idea struck me as we rolled over the abandoned train tracks. They were old and almost buried by plant growth.

"Hey... I know you don't want to talk about it, but has anyone ever found anything?

"No. Well, my friend's older brother said he found some human bones out there once, but nobody believed him."

"Oh. And where do people look?"

"Well, almost everybody goes to the lake." He pointed to the left of us, where we'd seen the teenagers heading earlier. "It's pretty deep back there but they figure that if there was another town, they would have lived by the lake, so...that's where they go."

"Well, you know what I would do? I would follow the train tracks. I mean, they look pretty old. And I don't know why they would lay them going back into those woods unless there was something back there, so that's where I'd go."

Jamie considered this and then nodded. "Yeah, I guess I could buy that. No one follows the tracks that way, though. That's where that kid that disappeared went."

I wasn't swayed.

I didn't bring up the Lost Town again until two weeks later. It was the weekend before we were moving home and my parents had a barbeque for the employees of dad's new store and some of our neighbors. Jamie and I hung out inside the house and played my N64 while we flirted pretty outrageously. There had been an unspoken sort of mutual attraction throughout the summer that no one had had the guts to act on. Since I was moving home in five days, there really was nothing left to lose.

Although his intentions were probably pure and genuine, I am embarrassed to say that mine were not. I thought that if I could make him want to impress me, he would agree to go looking for the

Lost Town. The legend had thoroughly consumed me. I had been to the local library every morning for the past week looking for more information on the town and had found nothing. But legends don't just come from nowhere! I was sure of it.

I knew if we didn't leave by 2pm we wouldn't have enough daylight to carry out my plan. I already had a backpack packed with water, a flashlight, a camera and a can of red spray-paint. I figured if we left the tracks we would need a way to find our way back to them. I thought I was so clever.

Nothing in that backpack made a damn bit of difference in the end. I was a fool.

I set my controller down and turned to look at Jamie.

"So...do you want to go out to the woods one last time?" I raised my eyebrow at him and smiled.

"Yeah!" He said excitedly and he jumped up off the couch. Then, embarrassed, he cast his eyes down at the floor. "Yeah, you know...if you want to, that's cool."

"Cool, let's go!" I grabbed his hand and ran out the front door, grabbing my strategically placed backpack on the way. Jamie didn't even notice it; he was walking faster than I was.

When we had gotten a decent way into the trees, Jamie turned around and looked briefly at my face before casting his eyes to the ground. He rubbed the back of his neck.

"I've actually, like, wanted to kiss you all summer."

I was stunned to silence, absolutely dumbfounded that Jamie had found the guts to say anything like this. I knew I needed to fill the awkward silence left in its wake, so I did the only thing I could think of - I leaned in and kissed him.

It was the awkward first kiss of two twelve year olds, but it made me feel warm and sent a flight of butterflies swirling into my stomach. So I actually really did like Jamie. How about that?

I let him go and his face was the same shade of red that I imagined mine was. He quickly changed the subject to how long he'd wanted to ask me out but that he didn't think I liked him back. We walked for awhile carrying on this conversation, him oblivious to his surroundings, me subtly leading the way.

It took him stumbling over the tracks to break off his monologue and finally notice the backpack. He looked at me like I'd punched him in the face.

"You can't be serious."

"Jamie, I know but look, this is the last time I'm going to see you in a really long time and I want to remember today! We will only be out for two hours max; we'll be back before they even realize we're gone!" Jamie stared at the tracks for a minute and seemed to be considering it all. I held my breath until he finally let out a deep sigh.

"Okay."

"Oh my God, Jamie, I-" He held up his finger, cutting me off.

"But we follow the tracks the entire time and we turn around after an hour."

"Okay!" I was so excited that I hugged him. It would be the first and last time I ever did.

As we walked, we talked about all sorts of mundane things, stopping only to make sure we were still on the tracks. It felt like we had only been walking for 45 minutes but when Jamie checked his watch, it had been 3 hours.

"That's weird....it hasn't been 3 hours. It says its 5 o'clock." He trailed off.

"I swear we left just after 2. It's can't be 5, dude, your watch is busted." I gave him a playful shove.

Jamie raised his eyebrow at me and smiled. "Even so, we should probably turn around. "

He wasn't wrong, the sun was setting. The shadows were long and looking around, I wondered if it really was 5 o'clock.

But I wasn't ready to give up just yet. As we had been walking, I'd noticed something taking shape off of our right; a large mass, maybe a quarter mile away. It was denser than the area around it and seemed to have clean, manmade lines.

"Jamie, look."

He turned. "Yeah, I was hoping you hadn't noticed it. It's a long way off though; we would never find the tracks again."

"Yes, we would, check it out!" I triumphantly pulled the spray paint out of my backpack. "It's for the trees."

He took the can and shook it, then made an experimental 'x' on a nearby tree.

"Ok, but I get to do the spraying." I didn't argue.

The closer we got to the mass, the more it took shape. First we could tell it was a building. Then we could tell it was church. By the time we got the front door, we were looking at a very old and dilapidated chapel. Remembering my camera, I took a picture of the wooden plaque over the door; whatever had been written on it had long ago worn away. We walked around the church in awe. The building was small, maybe 500 square feet. The windows were, surprisingly, all in tact but were so caked with dirt and grime that we couldn't see anything inside.

"How do we get in?" I asked quietly.

"I don't know, but we're going to figure it out! Wait until my brother hears about this. I mean, holy shit. Look at this place!" His excitement was contagious.

The front door had a pull handle but try as we might, we couldn't seem to open the door.

"Do you think it's locked?" I asked as I watched Jamie struggle with it.

"Yeah, maybe. I mean it must be. There was a door around back, though."

The door at the back was a lot more sympathetic and let us in with relative ease. We were standing in a small room with an old wooden desk attached to a wall. There was a small fire place and old portraits hung up around the tiny office. The people in the pictures were all standing in front of the same maroon background and were looking down at us disapprovingly. Books were scattered everywhere, most in a language I had never seen before. The floor was covered in dirt and a pair of old shoes were laying haphazardly in one corner.

"Whoa," I said in awe.

"Yeah, whoa." I looked over at Jamie who had a huge smile on his face. He was holding up a cross and a piece of paper.

"What is it?" I walked over to see.

"It's a list of names. There's like 60 people on this list. Maybe a town census?"

"Let me see." I pulled my flashlight out of my backpack and shined it on the parchment.

"Deepwood. Do you think that's the name of the town? All these names are crossed out. All except this one." I pointed to a name at the very bottom.

"Maybe it was the plague."

"You think it's a list of the dead?"

Jamie shrugged. "Makes as much sense as anything else."

I walked over to the desk and leaned against it. "Why do you think they left? I mean, look, there's a jacket or something on that chair, and shoes over there. The town pastor or whatever, he just took off and left everything like this?"

"Or died, "said Jamie as he folded the paper and put in into the back pack.

"Yeah, died... Either way it must have been creepy as hell to be alone in here." I stared at one of portraits for several long seconds; the young woman painted there seemed to be staring down at me with a very accusatory look. It made me incredibly uncomfortable.

I was so absorbed in the paintings that I didn't notice the slow creaking from overhead until the ceiling cracked loudly as it started to cave in. I screamed and covered my head, but the next thing I knew, I was laying on my back over the threshold of a door, Jamie on top of me protecting his head.

"Ah, thanks," I mumbled as I gently pushed Jamie off of me.

"Don't mention it." Jamie climbed to his feet and brushed himself off. I glanced behind him at the office, which was now filled floor to ceiling with decaying debris.

"That was our way out, Jamie."

"That's ok. We can unlock the front door now that we're inside. Or break one of the windows."

If the back office was unsettlingly, the chapel was downright disturbing.

Even though the grimy windows allowed very little sunlight in, I could make out eight rows of pews lining a narrow aisle and a tall podium at the front of the chapel.

Jamie and I stumbled around the small nave breaking windows on either side with pieces of wood we had found. The sun was still setting and I wondered how much of a difference the muted light would make. When I broke the last window on my side I turned back around to survey the chapel, disappointed that the lighting wasn't much better. The room itself seemed to repel light.

The wooden pews were completely rotted. In fact, the wood we had used to break the windows of the church were leg stands from the front row. The narrow aisle in between the rows of pews was littered with leaves and rotting wood. But that was nothing, nothing compared to what sat upon the alter.

It wasn't a podium, as I had thought earlier. It was a statue of the crucifixion – but unlike any I had ever seen before. The paint had been worn away on every part of the statue – except the blood of the crucifixion wounds, which stood bright and realistic, and seemed to be oozing before our very eyes. The only other surface left untouched by the decay of time was the face of Jesus. The details of his face were still so incredibly minute and perfect, and he had the same accusing eyes as the portraits in the pastor's office. He seemed to be staring directly at me and I could tell Jamie felt the same, though he was across the room from me.

The statue's stare awarded me an edge of panic, and I suddenly realized that we needed to leave. We weren't wanted here. I had the sudden feeling that we were trespassing on some sort of hallowed ground. We had found the church, we had documents proving we had been here – and now it was time to go.

I turned to Jamie to tell him so and could immediately tell that he did not share my feelings. He had been born and bred on these legends and nothing was going to tear him away from our discovery. I watched him walk over to grab the camera out of my bag. He took pictures of everything he deemed interesting, including the crucifixion statue, much to my unease.

I gave him several minutes before I said something.

"Jamie, I think we need to leave." I said in a low voice.

Jamie stopped and looked up, seeming to remember I was there.

"Are you kidding? This is what you came for! We have to bring home evidence, of all of it."

"It's going to be dark in half an hour. It's already hard to see in here…"

"Duh, that's why I'm using a flash. Hey, can you get a picture of me next to this creepy Jesus thing?"

"Um…I guess," I mumbled as I took the camera from him. I didn't even want to look at it, much less photograph it, but if it would help me get him out of here I was going to stomach it.

Jamie wrapped his arm around it just as I snapped the picture. "Don't touch it! Oh crap, why did you touch it? There's something off about that thing, Jamie. Can we fricking go now?!"

"Yeah, fine." Jamie walked over and picked up the backpack as I headed toward the front door.

I noticed there was no lock on it. I pushed against the door as hard as I could - it didn't budge. My heart sank; there wasn't even a handle or a knob. It was just a solid piece of wood with strange markings on it. Symbols I had never seen before.

"Jamie, the door is stuck," I said as I turned around to see him testing a piece of the floor with his foot.

"What are you doing?" I asked, hearing the edge of panic in my voice. He was still at the front of the chapel, a foot from the Jesus statue hopping back and forth from one part of the floor to another. The statue's eyes seemed to be only on him now.

"There's something under here. See?" I heard the floorboard creak under his left foot as he put weight on it.

"Jamie, don't."

"No, it's like, under the dirt right here, the floor is hallow," he kneeled down and starting digging through the thin layer of dirt, "it's like a trapdoor or something!"

And it was indeed a trap door. By the time I had walked the length of the pews, Jamie already had the edges dug halfway out.

"Let's just leave it and your brother and his friends can come back and see what it is, please, Jamie, I want to go." There was something wrong with this place. Terribly wrong. And the thought of spending one more minute here had me on the precipice of a panic attack, something I hadn't experienced in over a year.

I sat down against the front pew and put my head down. I heard a roaring in my ears and my breathing grew labored. I had to leave here, even without Jamie. I rocked back and forth for a few minutes as I tried to calm myself down. I would climb out a window and run – in any direction, it didn't matter.

"There's something here, under the church." Jamie's voice sounded a million miles away.

By the time I pulled myself together enough to lift my head, Jamie was knelt next to me.

"I didn't know you were claustrophobic." At least, that's what I think Jamie said. I better remember the horror I felt as I stared at the hole in the floor. Jamie had opened the trap door.

"Two minutes," Jamie said as he stood up. "We go down, we take a couple pictures of whatever's down there and we come right back up and leave. Just two minutes, Katie, that's all I'm asking."

I wanted to say no. I intended to. But I felt myself slowly nodding as Jamie pulled me to my feet. To this day I don't understand why I agreed. But I suppose that its better that what happened down there didn't happen to Jamie alone.

"We're going to come back with the story of a lifetime! What if there is valuable stuff down there or something? Old shit is always worth money. We could be rich! So rich that your family could stay here. You could buy the house you're living in and come to school with me in September."

I managed a small smile. Of all the things someone could think to buy with wealth, Jamie's first thought was to keep me here with him. And he was right, there could be anything down there and almost all old stuff was valuable. I took a deep breath.

"Okay, 2 minutes," I agreed.

As we leaned over the trapdoor and peered down, the first thing we noticed was an intense heat emanating upwards from the hole. The second was the strangely out of place spiral staircase leading into the depths below.

Jamie rolled the flashlight over to me with his foot and I picked it up as he pulled his lighter out of his pocket.

"Ladies first," he smirked at me.

I stared at him slack jawed.

"No way. You found this door, YOU go first. Between the black staircase and the heat, I feel like we're descending directly into hell. I am not going first." I crossed my arms and glared at him to reinforce my point.

Jamie simply shrugged and stepped onto the staircase.

I took several deep breaths as I watched his head disappear into the darkness below. I almost didn't follow him. I was still deciding when he yelled at me to shine the flashlight down the stairs so he could see.

I started down the stairs after him. They went down much farther than I thought, and it became warmer and warmer the further down we went.

When we finally reached the bottom, I was holding back what threatened to be a massive anxiety attack. We were farther beneath the church than I thought we'd be and it was hot, muggy and difficult to breathe.

Hoping to get this over with as fast as possible, I swung the flashlight around the chamber hoping to reveal its hidden treasure. What I saw there, I can never describe, though I have tried many times.

The room was entirely empty, save two things. One was a desk in the corner, much like the one in pastor's office. The second was another statue.

This one was roughly twelve feet tall, and remains to this day the most terrifying thing I've ever seen. To put it mildly, it was some sort of demon. It towered over us and as such I could only see the bottom of its jaw from where I was. It was looking directly ahead of it, at the staircase we had just descended. Its tail was long and swept around the entire room. There wasn't a lot of room to move. It had claws, like any modern depiction of a demon and as I moved around the chamber to view its profile, I noticed it had horns as well.

Neither Jamie nor I spoke as we shuffled around room, our backs to the wall as far away from the demon as physically possible. I stepped carefully over the tail as I made my way to its back and came around to the other side of the statue.

I couldn't take my eyes from it, I couldn't trust it. If the statue upstairs seemed to bleed, what could this one do? As I eyed the talons on the gigantic stone feet, Jamie broke the silence.

"Can you even believe this shit?" His voice was coming from the other side of the room. I searched the darkness for the weak glow of his lighter and was relieved to see it moving towards me. I turned my flashlight upward to shine it on the side of the demon's head. The horns had to be at least a foot tall. As I brought it down to see where Jamie was, I hit my arm on something hard.

"Ow, my head!" Jamie squeaked as my flashlight fell to the ground and rolled under the desk.

"Goddammit, Jamie," I whispered in a panic. I dropped to my knees and felt around under the desk, searching for the flashlight.

"What! It's not my fault you cracked me on the head."

I stood back up and swung the light around to see Jamie trying to relight his lighter – but it wasn't him that stopped me dead.

I will forever be frozen in that moment. I don't know why I couldn't speak, couldn't scream, couldn't move. All I could feel was my own intern decent into madness.

As I had moved the beam of light up to Jamie's face I had seen another face right next to his. A twisted, angry, soulless face – the demon's. The statue had bent down and turned to the side; its head mere inches from Jamie's. And it was staring at me. I can not describe its face, and I am not sure my mind will ever let me remember it in detail.

It shook me to my core in a literal sense. My body was having a dark, violent, visceral reaction to this impossibility. Jamie finally noticed the flashlight shaking in my hand and turned to see what I was looking at.

It wasn't until he started screaming that I was shaken from my paralysis – I dropped the flashlight, Jamie dropped everything else, and we ran.

We took the stairs 2 and 3 at a time, Jamie pushing me up ahead of him. Halfway up I slipped and we both went tumbling down halfway to the bottom. In that horrible moment we heard the grinding of stone against stone and we knew the statue was moving. Jamie screamed but I was mute, too horrified to make a sound. We got up and kept climbing, never taking our eyes off the small, dying light above us; our only salvation now.

We were almost to the top when we first heard it on the stairs. It was so large and heavy that the entire staircase shook with the impact. Terrified that the stairs would come crashing down and we would be left alone with it below, we jumped the last 3 steps.

Jamie pushed me up out of the opening. He climbed out after me and tried to slam the trapdoor shut but it was somehow stuck.

We could hear a deafening thunder on the staircase as the statue slowly climbed the steps. I helped Jamie try to push the trapdoor closed and for the first time noticed the symbols on the bottom of the wood – the same as those on the front door.

Before I could begin to comprehend this, I noticed the demon first penetrate the shaft of light on the staircase below. It was coming. Jamie saw it too and pulled me to a standing position while pointing at the front door.

We both ran at it as hard as we could – but when we hit it, it didn't budge. We tried again, but it was unsympathetic.

"Katie, the windows!" We ran to the closest one and tried to climb up the wall to get out, but the windows were too high.

The thunder from below was getting louder, closer. It was more than half way up the stairs…

We tried to climb on the rotting pews to reach the windows but they crumbled under our weight.

"I'll push you out, give me your foot!" Jamie yelled over the sound bellowing from below.

I shook my head. I wanted to, God, I wanted to. But I couldn't leave him. I couldn't leave Jamie to face that thing alone. We both looked over at the door again. Our only chance was to keep trying to break it down. We stumbled back into the aisle and ran at the front door with everything we had. I thought I felt it move. We backed up even further and ran at it again. This time the impact knocked me backwards into the aisle and Jamie barely stayed on his feet. He looked at me in horror and I turned around the see stone horns rising up from the darkness of the trapdoor, 3 feet from where I sat.

We were going to die here. I stood up, refusing to turn around again. I knew that the next step it took would bring its head into the room, and the thought of seeing its face again had me running at the door with every last bit of strength I had. Jamie reached it at the same time and I felt it give way as we crashed through the threshold and landed outside the church.

Jamie had picked me up off the ground before I could think to move and we were running toward the train tracks at an Olympic sprint. We could still hear the thundering on the stairs no matter how far we got from the church; every step echoed through the woods like a gunshot – until they stopped. It was here.

I had no idea if we had run in the right direction or if we would be forever lost in those woods. It was now dark outside and the temperature was dropping fast. I was beginning to panic that we would never find the train tracks when I noticed Jamie wasn't next to me anymore. I turned around in a panic to find him sprawled on the ground a few yards behind me- he had tripped over one of the rails. He was up and running down the tracks before I could even ask if he was okay. We ran until we couldn't anymore.

Our running eventually slowed to a jog and the jog to a walk. We hadn't spoken – neither of us had any idea what to say – and it wasn't until we had both gotten our breath back that one of us finally broke the silence.

"How long have we been on the tracks?" Jamie's voice had an edge of barely suppressed fear. I looked at his wrist, and noticed his watch was missing.

"It didn't take us this long to get, to get…to find that place. Or did it? Do you think maybe we went the wrong way?" Jamie asked hesitantly.

I couldn't afford to think like that. If we had somehow gotten turned around and ran the wrong way down the train tracks, than we were deeper into the woods than ever.

"No. We went the right way," I said to convince myself.

"That thing," Jamie started, "I thought it was a statue. But maybe it was some crazy undiscovered giant reptile that was, like, hibernating and we woke it up."

So we were going to delude ourselves into thinking that there was a scientific explanation for this. I understood why but I just couldn't accept it.

"Yeah," I said slowly, "did you, um, did you see the weird writing on the front door? It was on the trapdoor, too. Do you think it was keeping it down there? Because, Jamie, all those doors are open now."

"Well, if it's an animal, words mean nothing to it, anyway."

"Yeah, if…" I trailed off hoping he would challenge my implication. He didn't.

I could tell this was something Jamie's mind wouldn't accept. But he hadn't seen its face, not like I had. It was no animal. It was made of stone. It was something sinister and anciently evil and it had seen me, had seen right down into my soul. It was aware of me and I was aware of it. And now, it was free. Whatever had been keeping it beneath the church has been awkwardly destroyed by Jamie and me. That thing was free to walk the woods and go God knows where.

We walked in silence for another half hour until Jamie suddenly stopped short and started yelling.

"Here! We're here!" He booked it down the tracks toward a swarm of flashlights and I followed close behind him. As soon as Jamie reached his parents he collapsed, while I ran into my mother's arms and cried like a child. I couldn't hold it together any longer.

The police report says we were found at 4am – by our sense of time about 3 hours after the sun had set. We had spent less than an hour in the chapel and yet we seemed to have lost 10 hours there. We never told anyone where we had actually been, or that we had found the lost city of Deepwood. We simply said we went for a walk to the lake and got lost in the woods.

My family left Middlesbrough the following Monday – two days ahead of schedule. My father had another store to open and there was really no reason to wait. Jamie didn't come to say goodbye to me and after we left Middlesbrough I never saw him again. I kept a copy of the police report to remember him.

Over the following year, Middlesbrough slowly disappeared. At first, I could just feel the memory fading unnaturally from my mind. My parents couldn't remember that we had ever been there, which scared me more than anything else. I taped the police report to the ceiling over my bed so that Jamie would be the first and last thing I thought about everyday.

Then, the Middlesbrough city website disappeared as did that of the local paper and the town's two public schools.

The store my dad helped open in 2002 also disappeared from the company's website. After that I could never find any mention of Middlesbrough anywhere online ever again.

Over the years, I searched public records for Jamie's full name and found nothing. I hired someone to illegally search private records and he came up empty too. In the end, the only proof that Jamie ever existed at all was the police report with his name on it.

And then nothing was left. One day the paper I had had taped to my ceiling for so many years was blank. I remember what it was and what it looked like before, but now it's just an old weathered piece of blank paper.

All that remains of Middlesbrough and the people who lived there are my memories. And this is why I am writing this story down and uploading it to the internet. Once it's on the internet, it can never die, right? Or perhaps one day it will just disappear and you won't remember ever seeing it and I won't remember ever writing it.

And I can only hope that this ended with Middlesbrough. If it has moved on to other towns, who would know? Who would even remember?

I wish I had answers. But all I have are questions.

THE LOST TOWN OF DEEPWOOD
PART 2

Harrisburg is an antiquated, yet charming Pennsylvanian town on the Susquehanna River with roots reaching back into the 18th century. At least, that's what the tourism brochure read. I'd really have to take their word for it. I had researched a lot of Pennsylvania townships in the last year, but this wasn't one of them.

I handed the brochure back to the tall, red faced girl behind the hotel desk. She sniffed loudly as she took it and unceremoniously slid my credit card back across the counter at me.

"Thanks," I muttered.

The girl dropped a brass key on the counter which I eyed with suspicion. I hadn't seen a hotel with actual brass keys since I was a kid. I didn't know if it was my limited funds or Harrisburg's "antiquated charm" at work, but either way, it sent an involuntary shudder down my spine.

"Room 217. Check out's at 10." The girl said, wiping her small, watery eyes with the back of her sleeve.

I picked up my luggage and shoved off to find my room.

Eager to be done with it, I hadn't bothered to ask where to find room 217. When I finally located it on the other side of the building, I was exhausted and ready for whatever awaited me on the other side of the door. It was as you'd suspect: dated, droll and dusty. I took a short shower and spread my maps out on the painfully flat yet somehow still lumpy hotel mattress.

It was strange to be back in Pennsylvania after all these years. Honestly, I was just happy it was still here. I had spent years trying to pretend I'd dreamed it all. Trying to convince myself that I'd had a very vivid psychotic breakdown and I'd never actually been to Pennsylvania at all. And I might have believed it too - if it weren't for Jamie.

He was as real to me as the face in the mirror. I couldn't have dreamed him up if I'd wanted to. And if he had been real, than so had everything else. The Damned Church, the Demon and the hell

I'd brought down on Middlesbrough. How many more had died since then? I needed to see for myself. I needed to prove I wasn't crazy, even if doing it meant I would have to face the consequences of my actions - the death.

I stared at my notes and topographical maps until my vision began to blur. I'd been researching and preparing for this trip for a year and yet, here I was, in Pennsylvania, still with no real direction.

It had been thirteen years since I'd stepped foot in this state and only for one of them had I considered coming back.

I'd lived only half a life for the last decade, slowly suffocating under the heavy, pungent cloak of guilt. Usually, I could escape it in Ambien laced dreams or when I was utterly black out drunk - which is an easy order to fill when you work in a bar. But a year ago, my tricks had abruptly stopped working and it had been too long since I'd come up for air. I'd known it was time to go back.

I spent an hour trying to find a comfortable position on the worn-out hotel mattress. When that failed, I picked up the maps again and studied their details, though I'd memorized them all. I suppose I was waiting for something to just click, some small detail I'd overlooked that would suddenly make all the difference; a clue as clear as daybreak that had been in front of me all along. But none came and when I woke again it was buried under a pile of legal pads and maps and suffering a sore back.

I showered again, not trusting the comforter, and reluctantly drank the motor oil that passed for breakfast blend coffee. I packed up my research, checked out of the hotel and sat in my car watching the sun slowly brighten the populated downtown area. At least the creature hadn't made its way here; this city had a population of around 50,000. But how many other cities with similar populations were gone because of me? It wasn't something I wanted an answer to.

Since I had no other data to go on, my plan was to drive to the least populated areas and see if what wasn't there would give me a clue to what had once been. Basically, I was looking for an area that by all logic should have a city – but didn't.

I put the Ford Focus in drive and headed west out of town. Half a day was spent driving to the middle of the state and another two days aimlessly driving around central Pennsylvania looking for something familiar; a mountain, a water tower, a road, *anything*. But it was as if I'd never lived here at all.

On the fourth morning, discouraged and frustrated, I checked out of yet another shitty motel. I only had three more days before my flight back to Arizona and so far the trip had been utterly useless.

The man at the front desk took my key and gestured toward the "continental breakfast" of prepackaged muffins and horse-piss coffee.

"No thanks," I grumbled.

"Wheryeadded?"

"Huh?" I raised an eyebrow at him.

"Where ye headed?" He repeated, more slowly. I couldn't place his accent; the closest I could get was maybe southern.

"Oh, ah, I don't know."

"Well, if yer 'eaded down the 320, gas up before ya leave town. There ain't no gas stations or towns between here and Lannenburg."

"But…that's like 90 miles away."

"Yep, never understood it myself. People get stuck on that road all the time, blowin' tires and runnin' outta gas. I don't know why the government hasn't done sumthin about that."

"Because they're broke!" Someone yelled from the back office.

"Yep, that's it, most likely. The state ain't got money for it."

"I'll get gas before I go," I promised and received an approving nod in return.

I practically ran out the door. For days I'd been looking for the out-of-place, the not-quite-right, the bizarre and this was…well, it was odd, at least. And it was all I had.

I gassed up before I left town and followed the signs to the 320. As promised, it was nothing but dark asphalt for miles. No exits, rest stops, signs or ever mile markers. This was it. It just had to be.

Since there was no one else on the road, I drove well under the speed limit taking in every detail. Eventually I began to notice that periodically there would a gap. Not in the foliage, but in the coloring of it.

Every so often, a grove of trees would be duller, sicker. It was something you'd only notice if you were looking for it. So the creature, as I'd taken to calling it, could technically "give life" (in the process of filing in the hole of previous existence) but not very good life. The fauna in these spots was weaker and bore dull, almost muted coloring.

I continued noting these spots until I couldn't count them anymore. These had likely been cities or homes of people with lives, families, futures, all taken from them because of me. I felt the panic begin to claim the edges of my vision and quickly popped a Xanax. My panic attacks had become unbearable after Middlesbrough. I suffered from them still. The edges of my vision got hazy and I was able to relax a fraction.

At some point, I processed the presence of the dilapidated railroad tracks running parallel to the road. I'd noticed them early on, but my mind had hidden the significance of this until now. They may not have been *the* tracks, but to me, it was a sign that I was on the right track (so to speak).

I was close. I had to be. And if Lannenburg was still there, that meant the creature hadn't made it that far yet.

I somehow knew - like I knew that I'd once lived somewhere off this road - that the creature had been moving north. But it hadn't claimed Lannenburg yet. Why? Was it satiated? Had it left the area? Or was it just slow moving? Whatever the answer, I felt I'd learn it in Lannenburg.

As I reached the outskirts of the city, I saw my first road sign since I'd merged onto the 320.

Lannenburg

Next 17 exits

I decided to take the exit that would get me into the heart of downtown Lannenburg, if there was one. I hadn't researched the city of Lannenburg either, thinking it was too far north to matter. And yet, here I was.

The downtown area began to take shape off my right like the Damned Church had in the woods so long ago. But I didn't need spray paint to find my way anymore. I exited the highway and drove around the cityscape until I found a centrally located hotel that I could afford. I parked and heaved my bags out of the car, hoping they had vacancy.

They did, I was told by the overly flirty college senior behind the front desk, slinging his guitar behind his back.

"Do you have wifi?" I asked as he handed me the key card.

"We do, but there's a $10 a day charge for the password."

"Damn." I was on an extremely tight budget.

"But I can give it to you for free if..." He let his voice trail off suggestively.

"If what?" I raised a skeptical eyebrow at him.

"If you let me write a song about you-"he righted my credit card receipt so he could read it "-Caitlin."

I sighed. "Ok, yeah, fine." At this point there wasn't much I'd say no to. I was going on four days of restless sleep.

He eagerly gave me the password and I retired to my room, first floor, thankfully. I took out my shitty laptop, connected to the hotel's equally shitty wifi and pulled up the Wikipedia page for Lannenburg.

It was a larger city for this part of the state, around 55,000 residents, mostly due to the fact that Lannenburg hosted a state university. It was a progressive, young, educated town filled with hipsters and young professionals. Where to even begin?

I threw my notes, my phone and my GPS in my backpack and decided to start with the front desk of the motel, much to my own dread.

The college kid who'd checked me in was strumming chords on his guitar and softly humming.

"Excuse me."

He looked up at me and winked. "You're pretty eager, foxy lady. I like that. But songs take time to write, even for the most talented-"

"Yeah, actually, I was just wondering, where can I find the university?" I interrupted - suppressing an eye roll.

"Mama, this whole city is a campus! I mean, where'd you wanna go? You a new student? I'll show you around. I get off in-"

"No, I'd like to find the, ah, the-" This had been a horrible mistake. *Think of something quick, genius.* "-admissions office. I need to talk to admissions."

"Ah, well, that's about half a mile down Rooker Street. That's the one-"

"-running in front of the building, got it, thanks."

He started to say something else, perhaps which way to go down Rooker, but I was already out the door. Not knowing what else to do – and wanting to get as far from the poor kid as possible – I picked a direction and started walking.

Even though it was May, I was still freezing. I hadn't been built for the far north and my blood had thinned out living in Arizona. With my backpack and my age I probably would have passed for any other college student on campus – if it wasn't for the hoodie I had pulled tightly around me.

I envied them all. Kids just a year or two younger than me going to classes, hanging out with their friends, making stupid yet amusing mistakes. It could have been me, once. But I hadn't grown up like them. Even since Middlesbrough I had struggled with school and life in general. I couldn't focus, I couldn't laugh; I became a sarcastic, guilt-ridden introvert and I lost all my friends. Then my dad died and my mom started to look at me differently. I stopped talking about Middlesbrough the day I heard the word "hospital" whispered to my mother by a psychiatrist.

Even though I stopped trying to prove it had all been real, my mother never really saw me as her little girl again. I'd moved out at 18 and lived alone for years, working in an English pub, trying to forget how many people were probably dead because me - including Jamie, the knife that dug the deepest.

I walked the downtown area all day. I didn't know what I was doing, where I was going, who I should approach, or what I should ask them - I just knew I was in the right place. I'd been drawn here for a reason; I felt it in my gut. This was where I was supposed to be. But for the fifth time in as many days I had to ask myself: what now?

I suppose I could have spent days wondering around Lannenburg. I could have left empty handed and never known what happened all those years ago. I could have never found him. But, as fate would have it, it only took half a day to find what I was looking for.

It was well past noon and I had stopped at a small café to eat a sandwich. Since the restaurant was packed wall to wall with students, I went outside and leaned against the brick wall by the door.

I suppose I noticed it because it was so brightly colored. Or maybe because it was the only piece of litter I had seen all morning. Or, just maybe, it was simply because I was supposed to. But for whatever the reason, when a bright red flyer blew past my feet, I reached out to step on it.

Curious, I bent down to pick it up and read the heading:

Tethen History Museum – Lannenburg, PA
Upcoming Exhibitions
13th-14th Century Judeo-Christian Relics and Artifacts

Below that was a blurb about the museum, nothing too interesting. And below *that* was a description of the exhibits to be unveiled.

I skimmed down the list quickly seeing little of interest – until the very bottom.

Statue of the Demon Metaraxes

My mouth fell open. It was too much of a coincidence, nothing to be ignored. I checked the date on the flyer. May 2nd 2014: 3 weeks ago. I threw the rest of my sandwich in the trash and took off. I'd seen the museum that morning and I knew where exactly where to find it.

It was only three blocks away and I got there in less than five minutes, flew up the building steps and stumbled straight to the cashier window.

"Student ID, please." The old man said, flatly.

"I'm not a student."

"Well, you look-"

"How much?"

"Eleven dollars." I was gladly willing to pay.

I didn't stop to grab a map, instead joining a tour group already in progress. The museum, I could tell, was a veritable labyrinth and I certainly didn't want to get lost, not in here, not with that thing - if indeed, it really was what I half hoped, half dreaded it could be.

It took the longest twenty minutes of my life, but we finally came to the room I'd been waiting for.

"Now behind this door is our newest exhibition on ancient Judeo-Christian artifacts. Please do not try to touch anything or you will be escorted out. These pieces are centuries old and may be damaged by the lightest touch."

If you have behind that door what I suspect you do, than I highly doubt it.

"Also, please no flash photography."

My heart beat a million miles a minute as the docent opened the double doors and my group was shuffled in. I lingered toward the back, letting everyone go in front of me. I had come thousands of miles and done months of research to find that statue, to prove I wasn't insane, yet when the time came to possibly face my nightmare, I was hesitant. Finally I was the last and the docent had to wave me in with a polite but impatient hand.

There were about a hundred things in that room. All sorts of things, really: sculptures, paintings, pottery, and even other statues. But I only had eyes for the thing in the middle.

It was larger than I remembered. Not the twelve feet I had guessed, it was actually closer to twenty. But every detail of its face and body was exactly as I'd remembered, though it was positioned differently now.

In the church, all those years ago, it had seemed as if it was standing, waiting yet content. But now it was positioned as if ready to leap off the stone square that it stood upon, its tail was paused in midair, instead of wrapped idly around it's legs as it'd been before.

Though it was taller than I'd remembered, I could at least see its face this time. It wasn't particularly scary, just an empty, stony face, far from the hungry, animated one it became when it woke.

And like the crucifixion statue in the Damned Church, it had eyes only for me.

The rest of my group took photos, oo-ing and ah-ing as they made their way around the room. I stood directly where I was, against the now closed door, going no further. The docent walked around the room, discussing notable pieces of the collection and I only moved from the door when she finally stood before the creature.

"And, finally, the jewel of this exhibition: a granite statue from the 14th century. This is a representation of Metaraxes, a lesser known demon of Christian mythology. It is unique in its size as well as its crisp detail, especially for something so old. Our conservationists are unable to discover its place of origin or creator."

I edged closer and closer to the red velvet rope. Its eyes followed my every step. The room seemed to grow hotter.

The docent moved to the side so people could get pictures in front of the statue. Though I couldn't blame them, I barely kept from yelling. This was madness.

The stone platform on which the demon stood was covered in red velvet, which pooled at the creature's feet. It hid the words inscribed on the front of the granite stand that Jamie and I couldn't read those many years ago.

The docent droned on about nothing and I read the description plaque.

14th Century representation of the Demon Metaraxes
Artist Unknown

No shit.

And then I saw what I didn't know I'd been looking for – the triangles. The symbols I would never forget, etched into the doors of the Damned Church. And once I found one, I found another and another. There were half a dozen of them. *So that's how they're doing it.* They (whoever "they" were) had placed wards all around the base of the creatures stand.

The museum not only knew what this thing was, they knew about the sigils on the doors of the Damned Church and were *using* them to trap the statue here. The revelation was like a punch to the face. Someone was aware of what this statue really was and was blatantly risking innocent lives anyway. It was insane.

In a panic, I turned to find the docent and saw her conversing politely with an elderly couple.

"Excuse me!" I interrupted loudly.

"Yes?" She failed to mask her irritation at my rudeness.

"Where did the museum acquire this statue?"

"This piece is on loan from a private collection."

"Whose?"

"It belongs to Jameson Scott." The docent, feeling the exchange was over, turned back to finish her conversation.

Jameson Scott. I knew that name, but from where? As our group began to move out of the room I took one last look at the creature – Metaraxes – and shuddered. Its eyes had never strayed from me. I took my phone out and pulled up a Wikipedia page on Jameson Scott. I had to know who could be this stupid.

He was young – my age – but wealthy, had his own company and well known in the tech industry for multiple inventions. The words "brilliant", "pioneer" and "industry leader" were scattered throughout his Wikipedia page, which had no picture. At the end of the article, under "Personal Life", was a short paragraph about his interest in symbolism and ancient artifacts.

I shook my head as my group was herded into the museum's gift shop. What did he want with the statue? How had he acquired it? And how did he know about the wards? None of it made sense. I wandered through the gift shop idly picking up trinkets and wondering just what to do. Should I warn the docent? The curator? Or did this Scott person know what he was doing. Were the wards enough? Somehow, I didn't think so.

"Are you going to the lecture tonight?" Some one asked from behind me.

I swung around, my backpack nearly taking out a postcard stand as I did.

"Oh! Sorry, I thought you were someone else." The redheaded girl turned to leave.

"What lecture?" I asked before she could get away.

"The lecture our guide was talking about?" I stared at her blankly. "Jameson Scott's lecture on the exhibit?"

"He's in town?"

"Yeah, that's what she said," the girl said, flippantly. "You should go, he's really hot."

She turned to leave.

"Wait- where is the lecture again?

"The auditorium in the history building? Building E?" She said, as if I should have known. And I guess she wasn't wrong. I was only a few years older than her and I looked like a college student. Apparently everyone thought so.

"Thanks!" I yelled after her as she walked off with her giggling friend.

I would definitely be there. I had a few things to say to this guy and I wasn't leaving Pennsylvania until I did.

I sat in the back of the auditorium, as was my custom. The room was filled wall to wall with people, faculty and students alike. An empty podium sat in the front and a tall, blonde haired security guard stood to its left. He had a gun on his hip and his hands were folded behind his back. Maybe he wasn't a security guard after all. I was pretty sure state campuses were gun free, which meant he was with somebody important. Jameson Scott, no doubt.

The guard stared straight ahead, his eyes boring a hole into the wall behind me. Lots of things about him made me uneasy.

The murmurs and whispers died down a moment later when a thin, attractive man walked purposefully onto the stage.

"Good evening," he began. He graced the room with a smile that couldn't fool me. The emotion didn't quite reach his eyes; if anything he looked like the most stressed out and tired 25 year old I'd ever seen.

"My name is Jameson Scott. I am here to speak to you tonight about a few ancient and interesting items I have collected over the years. I'm sorry, but I will not be answering questions about my company, our newest patents or my personal charities."

Easy, Christian Grey. I rolled my eyes.

There were a few disappointed groans from the audience but Jameson Scott smiled and directly a flirtatious wink at no one in particular. He was an alarmingly charming man.

"I have been interested in ancient relics, particularly those of religious significance, for many years. Since I was quite young, actually. A somewhat traumatic experience played the catalyst and I've been studying and collecting ever since. I'll begin with some of my more well known pieces and then move on to the more exotic. "

Scott began his lecture on a bowl from Mesopotamia that was supposed to bestow on the user unnaturally long life – as long as you drank from it only water siphoned from the bottom of the Euphrates River. He spoke extensively about several other, equally uninteresting, artifacts before finally coming to the only one I cared about – the statue.

"Please study this photo for a minute." Scott clicked to the next slide in his sideshow and the demon statue appeared against a blood-red background, as imposing and terrifying as it was in real life. A blanket of heavy, uncomfortable air descended on the room as people averted their eyes from the screen and mumbled, uncertainly. I didn't take my eyes off of it.

"This is the piece I spent most of my life trying to locate. May I introduce to you, the demon Metaraxes." He paused for a minute and clicked to the next slide, a Dante-esque depiction of Hell.

"Metaraxes belongs to the second hierarchy of demons, though he is virtually unknown – and this is simply because of his nature. Metaraxes doesn't kill or possess. He doesn't vie for power, bring darkness into the hearts of men or try to influence innocence. Metaraxes eats. But he eats more than the flesh of man; he eats their homes, their histories and their souls. If you were to be eaten by Metaraxes it would be as if you'd never existed at all. No one would remember you and the now empty piece of life you had carved out for yourself in the world would fill in as if you were never there. Everything that was you or ever would be you is gone."

Jameson Scott paused artfully to let his words wash over the audience; every soul in the room hanging on every syllable. I suppose it really was quite interesting, if you didn't know the heartbreaking truth of it – which I knew he *did*. For someone hailed as a "genius" it seemed utterly reckless of him to romanticize all this. I crossed my arms and slumped lower in my chair. When this was over, one way or another, Jameson Scott and I would be having a conversation.

"And this is why Metaraxes is an unknown. There is no one to speak his name or his deeds, alive or dead. Or there wasn't, for many centuries."

"At some point in history, Metaraxes grew tired of being unknown and un-worshipped. He proclaimed that those who prayed to him and brought him sacrifice would not only be spared and but also given gifts of everlasting youth and resilience – that which he had stolen from others. It is believed that several ancient civilizations took him up on his offer; they sang his songs, built his temples and created beautiful artwork in his likeness - such as the one in your museum - to praise the demon and reap his gifts."

"And this would have gone on for many years until a name was called that refused to be sacrificed. Metaraxes choose his tribute selectively but eventually a name would come up of someone rich or in power and that person would maneuver out of it, or simply commit suicide. In these instances, Metaraxes would grow angry and eat the city and all the people therein, leaving no trace that he, or they, had ever existed. This would have happens many times over the centuries."

Now this was interesting. The creature could be tamed, like a pet, and as long as you gave it the treat it wanted, you would be not only saved but rewarded.

"Something else to consider is that no one ever knew how often Metaraxes called a name. Since the person would be absorbed by the demon, no one would ever remember they had existed at all. It could have been one person a year or five a day and no one would know but the demon himself."

"You will find mentions of Metaraxes scattered in religious texts dating back as far as 1700 BC but this statue is rare in that it is the only known likeness of him ever to be found."

Jameson graced the many hands in the air with another tired smile and said, "I'm sorry but no questions, tonight. If you haven't yet had a chance to see the statue of Metaraxes, I encourage you to experience it before it is shipped to New York next month. "

Then, without any ceremony at all, Jameson Scott simply walked off stage and the lecture was over. His security guard, who I realized was more likely a bodyguard, stepped forward to block several girls who jumped the stage to follow his boss. With him busy, I knew I had a chance.

As the throng of people pressed forward to the upper exits, I fell back and went out the rear. I sprinted out of the building and rounded the corner hoping to see what I'd gambled was there.

And it was. Jameson Scott was climbing into the back of a white SUV when I spotted him. He glanced in my direction at the sound of his name but then shut the door and rolled down the window as the SUV began to pull away. I threw a Hail Mary.

"Your wards on that demon will never hold!" My voice echoed down the alleyway.

The brake lights came on immediately, but no one exited the car. Taking it as an invitation, I ran up to his window.

For a mere 25 years old, he sure looked like he'd seen some shit. His lined, pale, yet attractive face no longer carried a tired look, but a surprised one. I bent over to catch my breath.

He didn't speak, but opened the door and scooted over. I climbed in.

"Who may I have the pleasure?"

"Caitlin Ross," I held out a shaky hand. His surprise seemed to turn to shock.

"Caitlin Ross." He said slowly, with a strange inflection of reverence.

"Yes," I said, exasperated. "I'm Caitlin Ross. And your wards – they're bullshit."

He didn't even bother to ask how I'd known, which in turn, bothered me. He simply tapped the seat in front of him and his driver let go of the brake.

"Those wards have held for six years, Miss Ross. I assure you, they'll hold."

"You have no idea what you're dealing with here."

"Oh, I assure you I do." There was a hard, yet sad edge to his voice that suggested personal tragedy. I wondered if I'd misjudged him after all. "My apartments are only a block away. Perhaps we should speak more in my study. This isn't a conversation for anyone to overhear."

I noted the finality in his voice and, nodding, sat back in my seat. As long as I got to say what I'd come to say, I didn't care where we went.

We were let off at the corner where several men in his personal detail were already waiting. Scott escorted me into a private entrance and private elevator with only one button marked "Penthouse".

As soon as the elevator doors opened, one of his men ushered me into his cavernous study and the door was shut behind me. For whatever reason, Jameson entered from a different door a few minutes later, followed by his head bodyguard who'd been at the lecture. This one didn't like me one bit, barely concealing irritation and shades of panic when he saw me. He was older, clearly over 30, with dark blonde hair and a square jaw.

Jameson sat down behind his desk while I continued to stand. He gestured to an empty seat in front of him, but I shook my head. He gave a "suit yourself" shrug and turned to his bodyguard, whose eyes continued to bore angry holes through me as they did everything else he looked at. This was quickly becoming enemy territory.

"Scotch for me, Bannock. Anything for you, Caitlin?"

"Ah, no thanks..." I mumbled as the guard – Bannock – raked his hair back from his forehead in exasperation, I assumed at Scott's familiar use of my first name. *I'm no threat to your boss, buddy, if anything he is a threat to everyone else.*

I returned his icy glare, never wavering until his lips grew into a thin line and he curtly nodded to Jameson and left the room.

"First," Scott begin, "I want to establish-"

"Do you have any idea what you're doing?" I asked, suspending all platitudes.

Jameson leaned back cautiously in his chair, giving me a casual "go-on" gesture.

"Why would you bring that thing to a populated city? Why would you put it on display for all to see and touch? What sort of arrogance allows you to think that you could control it with a few poorly copied sigils?"

He had made no move during my short outburst other than to tent his fingers and stroke his jaw with his thumb.

"Which question would you like me to answer first?"

Just then the one called Bannock opened the door with a little too much force and brought his great lord and master a scotch. He turned to stand beside Jameson's desk, which seemed a natural and familiar spot for him.

"You may go, Eric." Jameson clipped without so much as looking at him. The guard didn't move and I continued to stare daggers at him. We engaged in our own little personal, silent standoff. He, like the statue, had eyes only for me, and they were filled with rage and fire.

"He can stay," I ground out, finally. Let him know I'm not afraid of him. If he was grateful for my help, he didn't show it.

"As you wish. Your question?"

I slid my eyes reluctantly back to Jameson. "How did you get it?"

"I bought it from the government."

"The government had it?" I asked, incredulously.

"The state of Pennsylvania. It appeared on government land, in the middle of nowhere, according to the surveyor who found it. They shipped it off to PSU who dated and appraised it and then they put it up for auction."

"They just *sold* it to the highest bidder?"

"Yes and why not? It's just a piece of granite to them and they needed the money. The state of Pennsylvania is suffering its own financial crisis. Though I suppose that's what happens when in essence 20% of the state just stops paying their taxes. It's a curious thing."

I winced. He didn't need to elaborate.

"Why did you buy it?" I demanded.

"Because I have personal history with Metaraxes. He has taken from me."

"He's taken from me, too, but I'm not parading him around in public, risking people's lives, their *souls* according to you."

"If you listened to my lecture, you would know why I do that."

I remained silent. Jameson sighed and leaned forward.

"You're right, Caitlin. The wards won't hold him, not forever, and we don't know what will. The only reason they're holding now is because I'm *giving* him what he wants."

I scoffed. "You assume that being exhibited in a museum satisfies the creature's desire for worship? And you're willing to stake people's lives on that?"

"I am. That creature has not moved a millimeter since he came into my care. I've employed teams of symbologists and demonologists to research, test, and advise me on the safest course of action. And for our efforts, the statue has remained dormant."

"Yes, but it's not dead. You're going to kill someone, someday."

Jameson sprung up from his desk and was in front of me before I even had a chance to take a step back. His bodyguard took an almost involuntary step toward him but it was too late. Jameson was only inches from me and much more intimidating at eye level. Bannock seemed uneasy and ready to pounce if I tried anything. I didn't.

"What would you have me do, Caitlin? Would you like to take custody of it? What would you do with it? Tell me, and I'll consider it."

"Destroy it!"

He gave a sad, desperate bark of laughter. "Don't you think I tried that? Don't you think the first thing I did when I acquired it was try to kill it? I tried to incinerate it, hit it with a wrecking ball; I even ran it over with a tank. It won't be destroyed by any tools of man. And, believe me, Caitlin, I paid dearly for my attempts, almost everything I love is gone."

"Then I'd put it back where it came from." If the church was even still there and *if* I could find it.

"No one can do that." He laughed.

"Who did it kill? Who that you loved?" I don't know why I cared so much, but I couldn't let it go. I had to know.

Scott took a step back but held his ground.

"She was...she..." He trailed off.

"And just how did you escape the creature when it came for *you?*"

This question hit him physically, like a bullet. He leaned back against the desk, suddenly weaker, defeated and less imposing. Bannock visibly relaxed, his hand sliding off the handle of the gun I hadn't noticed was still holstered in his belt.

"That is a story for another time."

"Fine." But I wasn't backing down. "Then why you? Why are you the person who is qualified to own the statue?"

"Because I've seen its face. My fate is bound to it as surely as yours."

Jameson Scott rubbed his face in genuine exhaustion. If he hadn't been speaking the truth than he was a damn good actor. He looked up at me, finally, from hooded eyes that burned with some intense, unnamed emotion.

"And who did it take from you?"

"Jamie." I had nothing to hide and I wouldn't disrespect Jamie by hiding the truth. I raised my chin a little higher and crossed my arms. Scott's expression had turned milder, almost pensive and a sad smile graced his handsome face. The tension in the room abated, though Bannock was looking at me intently, his expression unchanged since the moment he'd walked into the room.

When Scott didn't reply, I decided it was now or never.

"I want to see it."

"No," he replied, quietly.

"Alone."

"No!" This time both Jameson and Bannock had spoken at the same time. I'd known he wouldn't let me go - he'd never let me near the statue again. I'd assumed this before I'd even met him, which is why I'd swiped the museum keycard off his desk as soon as I'd had the opportunity.

"Why not?" I asked him, anyway.

"Because he knows you."

"And you know he could break the wards if he wanted to."

"No, he could never get past the wards. They are perfectly drawn and blessed as they should be. But I won't risk your life." Jameson Scott suddenly seemed battle-weary, so much older than his 25 years.

"Don't even try it, Caitlin; he will take you if you do, and the only one who will ever remember you...is me." His plea was multilayered, intricately woven with threads of both deceit and familiarity. Once again, I was put ill at ease. There was only one more thing I wanted from this room.

"Who did it take from you and how? Tell me that and I'll leave Lannenburg in the morning and never come back." It was lie, but I was curious.

Jameson's eyes shifted to mine, perhaps to gauge if I meant what I said. He must have believed me, because his gaze drifted to the window and he answered my question.

"I took her from myself." It was an unsatisfying answer.

"Now leave," commanded his bodyguard before I'd had a chance to reply. Jameson stared at me as I took a step back from the desk. His eyes were again pregnant with an emotion I couldn't name, but it tread a line between longing and insanity. Perhaps desperate desire, perhaps insane desperation. Perhaps something in between.

"I will walk her out." Bannock bit as I made my escape out the door. *God, anyone but him.*

"No, I need you here, Andrews will see her out." The door closed behind me and I heard no more.

Andrews turned out to be an older man with a bald head and a white beard. He met me at the elevator and escorted me all the way to the ground floor, saying little.

"Do you need a ride somewhere?" He asked as we stepped out into the street.

"No, I can walk." He said no more, just turned around and let the private door shut behind him. Nice of him to ask, at least.

As I walked back to the museum, I had time to wonder just what in the hell I was doing. Why didn't I listen to Scott and just leave? What did I hope to gain by seeing that thing again? Couldn't I just trust that he seemed to have everything under control? Scott had the resources, the money, the people, and, most importantly, the motivation. He had lost someone too, after all, someone he loved, though how that had come to pass was not clear.

But I knew I had to see it again. Perhaps I could prove to him just how dangerous that thing was, regardless of the precautions he was taking. I needed to convince him to take the statue off display before more people died. It was madness, having it here. He was exposing innocent people, to a *demon* on a reckless gamble. If I could make the statue move just an inch or two, maybe even a turn of its head, it was be on the museum security tapes and I could prove the thing wasn't truly dormant. I read him as a pragmatic, reasonable man - he would remove the exhibit at once. I trusted that much, didn't I?

Once again I pulled up Jameson Scott's Wikipedia page. All I knew was that he was a pioneer in the tech industry, rich as a Rothschild and interested in 14th century Judeo-Christian artifacts. It didn't fit. It just didn't. ...unless Jameson Scott was telling the truth.

But even if he being honest about his past, Scott was still lying to me about something. Like everything else in the last week, I would have to trust my gut.

I arrived at the museum and walked around the giant building looking for the gift shop. At that moment I knew two things: the statue's room was next to the gift shop – and museums usually had nighttime security.

I slid Jameson's card through the reader next to the door and a light flashed green while the door emitted a soft click. I pushed it open and peered into the empty gift shop. Dim overheard lights gave the room an eerie and foreboding glow.

The room reminded me of another room from over ten years ago, a nave, darkened by dirty windows and a muted, setting sun. I was younger then, more innocent, and I'd had Jamie then.

What I wouldn't give to have him with me, now. What would he say? Would he trust Scott? Would he attempt to stir the creature for the greater good? Or would he say I was stupid for risking my life? Jameson was convinced the wards would hold. Would Jamie have been, too?

Whatever happened, I hope I didn't fail him.

I padded quietly through the dimly lit gift shop, pulling the straps of my backpack tighter over my shoulders like a security blanket. When I reached the opposite door, I leaned my head against it and tried to calm my rapidly beating heart.

Taking several deep breaths, I slid Scotts's keycard through the blinking card reader and was rewarded with a green flash and another soft click. The creature was right where I'd left it, as still as the statue it was pretending to be.

I took my time wandering around the room, my eyes never leaving Jameson Scott's prize exhibit. If the demon was as satisfied and successfully warded as Scott bragged it was, than the creature either wouldn't notice or wouldn't care about my presence. I was starting to hope he was right.

When I finally came around to face the statue, I approached it slowly and unbuckled the velvet rope with a shaky hand. I was so close to it now that all I could see when I looked up was the underside of its gigantic head. I suddenly wondered if years of schooling would help me read the words inscribed on the statue's stone platform. I bent down and started to pull up the velvet covering when I heard a quiet scrape above me, like stone on stone. It was a sound I'd heard before, in the soundtrack of my nightmares.

So I had been right all along, the statue wasn't dormant. It was a hollow victory. I dropped the velvet and backed away from the statue, trying to determine what had moved. Nothing had changed to my naked eye, but I know what I heard.

Bumping against the back wall, I decided to play a wild card. I needed it to move perceptibly if I wanted proof that the thing was still dangerous. I turned away from the demon and faced the wall, using an arm to brace myself. I couldn't believe I was doing this.

I pushed my chips all in.

"Do you really think I'm scared of you, after all these years?" I asked quietly, my voice echoing around the room like a gunshot. "You're just a piece of rock now. Harmless to me."

I held my breath and waited. Nothing.

Feeling both disappointed and relieved, I sighed and turned around, dropping the keycard as well as my jaw. Though it hadn't made a sound, the statue was now not only facing me, but leaning out, as far off its stone platform as it could. Its mouth was open and, almost imperceptibly, growing wider by the second.

"You can't leave your platform." I breathed, as much to myself as the creature. My whole body was shaking and I was quietly backing up, slowly, slowly to the door. I'd gotten what I'd come for, now it was time to leave.

It happened in the breath of a second. There was a sudden crack as the demon's tail whipped through the air behind it from one side to the other, as though it were not made of stone but of flesh and blood. The glass encasing it on either side shattered, the makeshift wall behind split in two and the velvet ropes came crashing down; one of the poles sent a sigil flying across the room.

I screamed like I'd never screamed before as the creatures neck seemed to stretch across the room toward me, one of its wards no longer effective. I turned my back on it and ran for the door realizing too late that the keycard now lay under a heap of rubble. I reached the double doors and tried to jerk them open, hoping they weren't locked from the other side. They were. The creature was once again still as stone, everything but its eyes, which followed my every move, hungrily. I beat on the door, yelling for security and wondering if I was doomed and which thought would be my last. In my hysterical panic I suddenly remembered how I had escaped this fate 13 years before. I stumbled back from the doors as much as I dared and ran at them, shoulder first.

They moved, creaked even, but ultimately laughed at my efforts. These were no rotten, decaying church doors. Crazed with fear I backed up to try again and this time just as my shoulder reached the door, it opened from the other side and I went spilling over on top of something hard – or someone.

He rolled over and I passively registered that I'd landed on an enraged Bannock. He was standing and pulling me up by the strap of my backpack before the door had even closed behind us.

Bannock struggled to say something, trying several times, but was too angry for words. I didn't care; I threw my arms around him just happy to be on the other side of the door.

He didn't hug me back, just froze stiff and waited for me to get off of him. When I finally pulled back, I pulled my hood down and looked him full in the face. He wore a decidedly guarded look.

"Did you see what it did?" I asked, pushing hair back from my face, "That thing is not dormant at all. Tell your boss that, and that it needs to be moved. Tonight, if possible."

In lieu of a response, Bannock grabbed my arm and headed toward the lobby. Since it was away from the exhibit room, I didn't care; he could take me to jail if he wanted, as long as Jameson Scott heard what happened here. I'd made my point to him and lived to tell the tale.

Or had I? I suddenly wondered. Honestly if I'd learned anything in that room, it had been that the creature hadn't forgotten me- the girl that got away. My life was a black mark on its record, an insult. And I had gone into its lair and challenged. What did I *think* was going to happen?

Of one thing I was abruptly certain: it wouldn't stop until it had my life. The creature would burn through a hundred cities, perhaps a thousand, to claim me. It had told me all of this somehow, hadn't it?

I suddenly realized my mistake. The creature had been dormant when I'd arrived in Lannenburg as it'd been dormant 13 years before in Deepwood. And once again I had awoken it from a harmless slumber. How many would pay the price this time? How many people had to die before the end?

125

Finally understanding the true cost of my arrogance, I let out a muffled cry and faltered, wondering with revulsion if perhaps I should just go back and face my fate.

"Wait." I coughed, trying to ply the guard's fingers from my arm.

Bannock suddenly spun me around and pinned me against a wall, his arms braced on either side of my head. My eyes snapped up at him in shock and I recoiled from what I saw there.

"What the fuck are you doing here?"

"I was, I was just-"

"Why did you come back, Katie? After all these fucking years?"

My objection died in my throat. But it couldn't be. It wasn't possible. And yet…somehow it was.

My legs gave out under me, but Jamie caught me on the way down. He was older than he should have been, and stronger than I'd ever thought the skinny kid from Middlesbrough could be. But his eyes hadn't changed, and it was Jamie all the same. Even his expressions were familiar to me, I realized. What I'd first thought was seething anger was actually just barely controlled fear. Had the creature killed me after all? Was I swirling in the dark abyss with Jamie and all the others who had been taken?

"Jamie?" My voice broke over his name.

"Christ, Katie, you need to leave now and never come back. Hell, leave the country if you can. He'll never stop looking for you now."

I couldn't register what he was saying. Who wouldn't? Leave what country? Jamie…how was Jamie here? He kept me pinned there; his hold rigid, his eyes desperate and little bit pissed off.

"Jamie," I tried again, "how did you…"

"How did I know you'd come here? When has the word 'no' ever kept you from something you wanted?"

"No, I mean how-"

"We'll take her from here, Bannock. " A voice behind him interrupted me.

126

Jamie slowly turned to face the three men, only one of which I recognized.

"This one has been too much trouble. I want her gone." Jamie returned with ice in his voice.

"Mr. Scott says we're not to take orders from you anymore, Bannock. Give her here."

Jamie suddenly pushed me out of the way and I went sliding across the floor, the wind knocked out of me. A rushing filled my ears as I tried desperately to catch my breath. When my hearing came back, Jamie was yelling at me.

"Go!"

I looked back to see two men down and Jamie struggling with the third. My sneakers struggled for purchase on the slick marble floor and when they finally found it, I was up and running toward the lobby on the wings of adrenaline. I suddenly heard a sound like a book slamming onto a table.

I spun around just as Jamie went down, clutching his shoulder. He fell on top of the man he'd been struggling with – who was now unconscious. Blood began to drip over his fingers and I went sliding across the floor as I tried to stop to double back for him.

Jamie started to say something but passed out mid sentence. His hand dropped from his shoulder and thin tendrils of blood began to race each other down his chest.

"Well, now that is impressive," Jameson Scott stepped forward from where he'd been leaning against the door. "And I'm not impressed by much at my age."

I stumbled over to Jamie, but Scott stopped me with a single click of his gun. He walked over and rested a foot on Jamie's chest. I froze where I was.

"I saw you take my keycard, you know. You played the role perfectly. In fact, *everything* went according to plan. Except him." Scott kicked Jamie in the ribs but he didn't make a sound.

"What do you want?" I spat.

"Your name came up. I want you to die."

"Why?"

Scott gave a pretentious scoff. "This isn't a James Bond movie, Miss Ross; I don't need to explain myself to you."

"But you will, won't you? You want me to know how clever you are." I was playing with fire but why not? We were far beyond caution now.

"Hmm, you're quite bright. There might have been a place for you on my staff...if things had been different."

"Don't flatter yourself. Why then? Why are you giving a demon what it wants? Didn't it kill someone you loved?"

"My daughter, actually. And why? It's my gift to a world I was born too late into. You know, I was fifty by the time the internet was invented - fifty! What sad irony then, that I was a technological genius. Oh but the universe does love its sick jokes. Do you realize I've single-handedly guided the history of modern technology? It's true. But I reached my seventies and then my eighties, and my vision began to fail, my hands would shake, I'd forget coding. I could barely manage to read at one point."

"I'd made millions, but I hadn't even started. I decided the world couldn't afford to lose me yet. So, I tracked down every piece of ancient lore I could that may help me reclaim my youth. Most of it was rubbish, of course, but I was desperate. I'd almost given up – until Metaraxes found me."

"I knew what he was as soon as I saw him. So I bought him and warded him using the sigils I'd read about in ancient text. Of course, there was an expensive trial and error period; many of my staff were killed in the process. But eventually, we discovered the right sigils. The first thing I did was track down the man whose name was etched into the granite at Metaraxes's feet. I presented him for sacrifice and I was rewarded."

"That was six years ago. I adopted a new name and started a new company. All was going well until your name came up about four years ago. It really stumped me because Metaraxes only desires those who are connected to him, somehow. I didn't know who you were and you're far from the only Caitlin Ross in the world. I did *try* several others. Metaraxes would take them, for certain, but the name never changed. I was getting desperate."

"So you can imagine how happy I am that you showed up on my doorstep. God is telling me that he approves of my methods and that I must stay alive for the good of humanity. My company is in the middle of revolutionizing surgical robotics, for Christ's sake! I will take a few lives to save a million."

Furious at his arrogance, I struggled to keep my voice level. "Don't lie to yourself, Scott; you're no hero, just an old man afraid to die."

"No, Caitlin, I'm just a man refusing to grow old. What can I say? I'm determined and resilient. I want to be young until the day I die."

"That's not resilience, that's vanity. Vanity is what you're buying with my life."

"There's always a price for social change, Miss Ross. And today, the cost is you. Oh, but you look upset. Don't be afraid of death, my dear, not for such a worthy cause."

"I'm not afraid of death and I don't care about your diabolical plan, I just want you to get to the goddamn point." Jamie's breathing was growing shallow and my voice dripped with animosity.

"As you wish." Scott nodded at something behind me and then there was darkness.

When I woke, I was lying on a cold marble floor, my brown mess of hair fanned out underneath me, stiff with dried blood and my wrists bound. I sat up slowly and tried to brush the hair out of my eyes. I knew where I was, there was no point in turning around to see it, but I did anyway.

It wasn't the fact that my name was engraved at the base of the statue that the velvet cloth had covered. It wasn't the wards, which had been moved from the demon's feet to the doors and walls of the room. It wasn't even the fact that the demon's head was turned as to be looking directly down at me.

No, what terrified me most in that room was the man leaning against the wall, hands bound behind his back, as condemned to death as I was.

The blood on his chest had dried and he was awake; his eyes only partly open, watching me with an unreadable expression.

"You look like shit, Jamie." I said matter-of-factly as I pulled myself up to lean against the base of the statue, the only thing nearby.

"I've been busy," He said, his mouth curling up into a sarcastic smile.

"I'm sorry I killed you. Again." I tried to smile back, if only to keep the tears at bay.

"Nah, we'll survive this."

"I admire your optimism, but look around." I rested my elbows on my knees and sunk my head into my arms.

"I lived through it once before didn't I?"

"Yeah about that - how?"

"About a week after you left things started disappearing around town: people, buildings, even roads. No one remembered them but me. Then one day, I woke up in an empty house. My dad and my brother were gone. So, I fled to the only place I knew was safe."

"The Damned Church."

Jamie shrugged. "I figured it was the one place the demon would never go. I don't know how long I lived there, but it felt like years. I slept at the church and traveled to nearby towns to steal what I needed to live. And then, one day, the towns were gone. All of them."

As he spoke, I watched him, memorizing every detail of his face. Even when I was nothing, I hoped something was left of me, a little piece that would remember him.

"So, I decided to find the thing. My dad was gone; my mom didn't remember me, and the only person who knew who I was lived a thousand miles away. So I went from town to town until I found it. It was just there; standing in the center of town. Nobody even thought it was weird."

"I was a pro at drawing sigils by then since I'd spent some much time at Deepwood, and sigils have to be perfect to work, so I tried to ward it. It would take a little while, but the statue always managed to break them. I'd find it a little further from its base every night. People didn't even seem to notice the statue had moved, what they did notice, however, was some kid loitering around their town.

Since I looked older, and the town was getting wary of me anyway, I joined the local police force and spent my nights on patrol downtown, keeping an eye on the thing, reapplying sigils. Occasionally, I would wake up outside and I'd know my wards had finally failed. Then I'd have to track it to a new town and start all over."

"Why didn't it just kill you?"

"I asked myself that until a few years ago when your name came up. I think it needed me - to find you. Ironically, in the end it didn't need me at all. You came anyway."

I thought about that and wondered for the first time if I actually *had* come back to prove myself sane. Had I really intended to kill it? Or prove I'd been right? Or had it actually been about Jamie all along?

"It took a long time, and a lot of towns," he continued, "but I finally figured out what I was doing wrong. A sigil will slow it down, but in order to stop it the ward needs to be blessed. And not just by anyone - by the second son of a Roman catholic, preferably from Assisi, Italy, or at least near the region. Don't ask me how I figured that out."

"So what happened to your second son from Assisi, Italy?"

"He disappeared."

"Shit." I pushed my hair back again with my bound wrists.

"Yeah. By that point I was a sheriff and I'd been a city over. I came back to town to find my exit missing. The statue was gone. And that's when Jameson Scott got a hold of it."

"And that's why were you protecting him?"

"You think I was protecting *him*? No, he was transparent about his intentions from the start. I applied to be on his detail but was denied - no name, no experience. I only got on because I was able to take out all of his bodyguards in a sort of hand to hand combat trial. Guess all those trips through the police academy finally paid off."

"Agreed. How does Jameson Scott know more about that statue than we do?"

" Because he had almost 80 people on his staff who did nothing but travel every corner of the globe looking for any scrap of information on 'Metaraxes'. We aren't the first ones to live to tell the tale. Just the first to stick around. I did all I could to keep people away from that thing. A name would be engraved on it one day, and a new name the next. It took me a long time to figure out what he was doing. And by then...your name had come up. He's became obsessed with you and I damned sure wasn't going to let him find you."

"Well that explains why you were mad when you saw me."

"Mad? Katie, I've never been more terrified in my life. I spent years leading him down false paths only to have you present yourself like a lamb for slaughter."

"I'm sorry, Jamie. I wasted all your fucking time. You spent 13 years trying to protect me and I spent all that time trying to forget you."

"Well, it's no less than I wanted for you. To forget about this place, and me."

I heard the familiar stone on stone sound from above me.

"Is there any chance of reasoning with him? Your boss, I mean?"

"Not likely," his voice was dark. "He fed his own daughter to that thing."

"He what?!"

"For the greater good, he said."

"God, Jamie, I don't want to die. I don't want *you* to die."

"You're not going to die here, not today."

I ignored his optimism. "Why do you think it hasn't killed us yet?"

Jamie sighed. "It's trying. Scott kept a close watch over his demon but I managed to get one thing by him. That statue is sitting on a sigil the size of a mini cooper. It's not blessed - but it's big."

"You're a brilliant bastard, James Karras."

"Well, I've sure had a lot of time." I heard a clicking sound and Jamie stood up, tossing a now worthless pair of handcuffs on the floor.

He walked over and stood me up; using whatever tool he had picked his own cuffs with to free me. I heard them click but when they fell to the floor all I heard with the loud grinding of stone on stone again. It was louder and longer this time.

"Don't look at it, Katie. Don't look up."

"Jamie..." I breathed, terrified. Suddenly, a face appeared behind Jamie. But this time, I wasn't hypnotized by it. Jamie saw the color drain from my face and grabbed me.

"Follow me- now!" He yelled, pushed me in front of him to the gift shop door. I heard more movement from behind us and turned around while Jamie typed a long sequence of numbers into the card reader keypad. The creature had turned its head and it was watching me. It was alive, as alive as it had ever been. The statue took a step off its platform which shook the museum floor. Its movements were silent, yet fluid and flexible, like a cartoon on mute.

"Jamie..."

"Working on it!" Suddenly the key pad flashed green and the door clicked open. Jamie drew a black marker out of his pocket and drew a long line down the middle of the sigil, negating it.

"What are you doing?!"

"Just trust me." Jamie pushed me out the door.

We slammed it behind us and tore across the gift shop to the exit. The door was locked. I turned around to tell Jamie as much but he was already hurling a table through the window. It shattered just as I saw the door on the other side of the room begin to bend as it was pushed in from the other side.

"How did you unlock that door?" I asked as we ran across the parking lot.

"Scott isn't the only one who's good with programming." Jamie yelled back.

I followed him to a black jeep sitting at the edge of the parking lot. We jumped in just as a loud bang echoed across the asphalt, god only knew what it meant. Jamie shoved his keys in the ignition and turned the car over. The beginning chords to "Highway to Hell" blasted from the speakers.

"Why not?" I shrugged as I turned it up. Jamie nodded and peeled out of the parking lot. We tore through town like the devil himself was chasing us - which wasn't far from the truth.

It was early, the first rays of sunlight streaming through the trees as we hit the highway. We hadn't gone more than 5 miles when a white SUV appeared behind us. It followed at a considerable distance.

"Why aren't they overtaking us?"

"Because this is what he wants. Scott knows where we're going."

"Where *are* we going?"

"Deepwood."

"Fuck." I said as I leaned back in the chair. But I trusted Jamie, so I didn't object. "Won't it take the creature days to make it there?" I asked, eyeing Jamie's speedometer, which was at 90.

"It doesn't always move like that. It sometimes travels on another plane. I can't explain it. Everything changes and warps around that thing, even time. That's why I'm about 8 years older than I should be."

He suddenly whipped off the road and headed for the tree line. The truck behind us did the same and we maneuvered randomly through the trees, though I figured Jamie knew where we were going. I held on for dear life and watched him expertly navigate the almost hostile terrain or downed trees and deep ditches.

"How far?" I asked after ten minutes.

"6 miles but you know how time is out here."

Did I ever. Four minutes yet somehow six miles later we bumped over a set of railroad tracks and arrived at the Damned Church, which looked smaller and more impotent than it did in my nightmares. The front door opened easily this time and I gave an involuntary shudder when I saw the Jesus statue - looking more judgmental now than ever before. The trapdoor was open.

"You lived here for years and you never closed the trap door?"

"Believe me, I tried." Jamie grabbed my hand and guided me to the hole in the floor. "We have to go down there."

"Fuck no." I snatched my hand away.

"It's the only way this will end, Katie."

"You've got to be kidding me," I muttered as I took the first reluctant step down.

"Wait," I suddenly stopped. "You said it wouldn't ever come back here."

"It would for you."

Jamie followed behind me and took the stairs down, on shaky step at a time. Jamie followed behind me, flashlight in hand. I didn't see it until right before we reached the bottom. The demon was already here waiting for us. It stood in the same position we'd first found him in 13 years before, though this time its face was not stone. The demon's eyes swept across the room in a wide arc, his tail was wrapped around the bottom of the staircase.

"If he was already down here, why couldn't we stay up there?" I whispered.

"He wasn't."

There were no wards to protect us now, and no where to run. I couldn't help thinking this was a bad plan.

"Well, he's here now, so let's go."

"We can't Katie. If we leave now, he will too."

"Well then what's your plan, Jamie?"

Jamie said nothing, just stared at the demon, who was now staring back at him. Suddenly I felt something like a tug, in the pit of my stomach. I stepped back, and then it happened again. I looked up into the creature's eyes, which had moved to mine and suddenly realized what was happening. There was another tug, harder this time, and I felt my mind, if not my body, being pulled toward the demon's head. A long black tongue jutted out to welcome me and the creature's mouth began to widen. So this was it. The nothingness.

The demon's mouth was so wide I could have simply walked into it, if I had a body. The blackness started to close in on all sides, creating a sort of tunnel vision and then, in a violent jolt, I was snapped back into my body, a perfect sigil drawn on my chest in black marker. The creature screamed, an earsplitting sound, and Jamie flung me over his shoulder before I had even reestablished my bearings. We were to the top of the staircase in under a minute, the demon still emitting a deafening wail.

"I'm sorry!" He yelled "I was sure it would come for me first!"

We burst into the nave, and Jamie, seeing our company before I did, pushed me across the aisle toward the crucifixion, which I took out as I fell. I scrambled back, kicking it away from me as I did. By the time I looked up, Jameson Scott was standing in front of the trapdoor, a gun to Jamie's head. His men hung back, but looked eager to get involved at a word from their boss.

"Get back down there, Miss Ross."

"Fuck you." My last word was drowned out by a loud cracking sound that echoed through the little church as the spiral staircase came crashing down below.

"Katie, don't-" Jamie caught a knee to the ribs, some of which I was pretty sure were already broken. I scrambled back further.

"There's- there's no staircase now. There's no way to get down there."

"Oh, sure there is." Scott sneered. His hired men laughed. "You're going to die either way. At least *this* way, you'll save his life. Metaraxes is trapped down there for the time being, so it's to the cellar you must go. Perhaps you shouldn't have injured him by breaking his bond *mid-feed.*"

"Katie," Jamie growled. "Don't be fucking stupid. Just run."

"Fuck no, Jamie. I didn't leave you in this place then and I wont now." It was time to pay my dues. I stood up to walk to the edge of the trapdoor. Perhaps, if fate was kind, I would die when I hit the floor thirty feet below.

I looked up at Jamie, intending my last words to be for him. I knew the moment he realized that intent.

Jamie jerked his body forward and threw himself and Scott into the dark hole between us.

"No!" I screamed as Scott's men scattered out the door. I skid over to the side of the hole, tripping over the smaller statue on the way.

"I'm here." It was a pained groan from Jamie, who was just barely clutching onto the side. Thanking every deity I knew of, I pulled him out of the hole and back into the nave. His wound was bleeding fresh blood and I knew we didn't have much time. I laid him on his back, as he started to slip in unconsciousness, applying pressure to his shoulder. A moan came from the trapdoor beside us.

"Help me. Please... I'm hurt." So Scott had survived the fall. I grimaced and pulled myself over to the edge to peer into the darkness below. I could see nothing but the creature was no longer screaming. My blood began to boil as I let Jameson Scott wail away his swan song.

"Please...it's staring at me, I can feel it. Please...name your price, I'll pay it. Just save me..."

I laughed. "Oh now, why would I do that, Mr. Scott? This is what you wanted, after all. You get to be young until the day you die."

Suddenly the trapdoor slammed shut, Jamie standing over it, as the entire building began to shake. The edges around the door grew bright, like molten metal before darkening like a blown out flame.

"Will it hold?" I yelled to Jamie over the increasingly loud earthquake. "Is it blessed?"

"Some say by God himself."

"I'd say that counts." I said to myself as I tried to stand up on the violently shaking floor.

Jamie hoisted me up next to him and ran for the door as bit of ceiling began to cave in. The door to the church swung open of its own volition before we got there and slammed shut behind us. The church came down in a cloud of dust and splintered wood. When all had settled, Jamie was barely conscious. I walked him to the car and pushed him into the passenger seat. He was out before I'd shut the door. I took one last look at the pile of rubble before climbing into the driver's seat and starting the car. I followed the same train tracks home that got us out of Deepwood when we were kids. I made it to the road without ever looking back.

I can tell you exactly how long Jameson Scott lived - 4 days. By the dawn of that forth day, he, and all of his inventions, abruptly disappeared from the world. There were a few I was sad to see go, like the rise of inductive charging and EyeGlass. You would have loved EyeGlass and you probably did, honestly. Contact lenses that were actually cameras: they put GoPro out of business. I could never afford it, but you may have had one. I miss those YouTube videos.

Jamie spent a month recovering from his gunshot wound. After he was released from the hospital, we spent a few weeks weighing our options. In the end, we decided to hunt down people like Jameson Scott and the powers they wielded. You don't know about them, and if we have our way, you never will. Due to Jamie's time with Scott, we have some good leads. We have a lot of blood on our hands to atone for, and a lifetime to do it in.

Deepwood is dead; only Jamie and I even know where it is, so the town dies with us. I wouldn't try to find it if I were you - I've changed a lot of details: names of towns, names of roads. Perhaps even *when* this all happened. I won't tell you and you don't want to know, anyway.

Somewhere, out in a hundred mile sea of trees and dirt lays the demon's door. It's still there, under a pile of rotting detritus that used to be a small church. The door may be found again someday, it may even be opened. But one thing is for damn sure: it sure as hell won't be because of me.

ABOUT THE AUTHOR

C.K.Walker lives in Phoenix, Arizona where she currently works a boring, white-collar day job. For new stories and content please visit: https://www.facebook.com/pages/C-K-Walker/1503387386575559.

Made in the USA
Lexington, KY
10 November 2016